Violet Fate

To
Wanda,

Love is for everyone

F. Sharon Swope

Genilee Parente

F. Sharon Swope
&
Genilee Swope Parente

Violet

Fate

An e-book edition of this book was published in 2015 by Spectacle Publishing Media Group, LLC.

For information address
Spectacle Publishing Media Group,
P.O. Box 295,
Lisle, NY 13797

First Spectacle Paperback Published 2015

Author photo by Aleda Johnson Powell

Cover design by Paola Pagano

978-1-938444-14-2

ACKNOWLEDGEMENTS

This is the third in our Fate series featuring Sam Osborne, and we've fallen in love with our character more and more with each book. That's why we decided it was time for him to have a love of his own.

We've also fallen in love with the readers of our books and the people who attend our book talks, signings and events. We hope all of you realize what one simple compliment or comment can mean to two women who have worked so hard to bring these characters to life.

Because we spent some time in our hometown of Edgerton, Ohio, this summer celebrating our first two books, we want to note how much we appreciate those who took time to stop by and give us their support. The encouragement and kind words bolstered us and gave us fuel for our journeys into the realm of our third and fourth books. In particular, thanks to Verna Wortkoetter, Penny Smith, Susan Herman of Susan's

Hair Flair, the Edgerton Public Library and Cindy Thiel of the Edgerton Earth, who made some of the miracles happen. We award the ribbon for traveling the furthest to a book event to Tara Sauernheimer and Sondra Lester. Their presence made the events even more meaningful and affirmed the power of family.

For this particular book, we needed to research kidnappings as well as how local police forces cooperate with each other and federal authorities. We turned straight to the source—the Federal Bureau of Investigations—with some of our questions and were delighted to find out they have an office to deal with authors. We also relied on help from Mark Swope, who we hope we're turning into a book research expert. We sent the book to a new friend, Johanna Muench, who spent a large amount of time during a busy period in her life sending back suggestions we found invaluable for improving our plot. Thanks also to Alice Sanders and Mary Carpenter from Victoria Park for helping us fine-tune details and for being such great friends.

We also doubt we'll ever have reason to stop acknowledging and thanking the head of our cheerleading team—Allyn Stotz. It was really fun sharing the spotlight with you in Edgerton this year.

As always, thanks to our husbands, Robert and Ray, for listening to us babble about book marketing woes and to the rest of our family, who give us love and patience. We are also grateful for Spectacle Publishing Media Group, our publisher and editorial team, who we feel strongly are in this wonderful world of writing with us—both through the improvements their creative teams make to our books and through their marketing support.

We began this journey with the hope that it would be rewarding and fun to work as a mother/daughter team in turning our ideas into something readers would enjoy. We had no idea how fulfilling it could be, and we can't wait for you to read the next chapters in Sam Osborne's life.

TABLE OF CONTENTS

PROLOGUE

"KILL THE KID."

He sat looking at the sleeping child, who was dressed in a clean white T-shirt and shorts that had grown dingy in the week they'd been here. The blond curls were cut tight to the head like those of the angels he remembered from childhood Sunday school lessons.

"Kill the kid."

The words echoed in his head, bouncing off the walls of the cottage and returning to haunt him. He couldn't make himself act, which wasn't like him at all.

Those three words had ended the conversation he'd had with his partner late last night on the phone. He knew she was right—they had to get rid of the evidence. Why the hell hadn't he done it yet? He had taken so many jobs in the last decade where getting rid of traces of the crime was the finishing act.

Something about this was different.

The rest of last night's conversation crowded in on his thoughts. He heard his partner's whining voice.

"Didn't everything go according to plan, just as I said it would? Didn't I tell you this would work? I have the money now; you have the transportation arranged. We'll be sipping tequila before you know it." Then: "You did take care of the plane, right?"

"Of course I took care of the plane," he'd said, irritation rising to the surface. He doubted she'd even noticed, and he knew she was just being her usual, thorough self. He sighed as he quelled his impatience and recited the details.

"We're meeting Donald at the airport Tuesday at six. He'll fly us to Puerto Vallarta, and we'll take a boat from there."

Her voice took on a cautionary note. "No questions asked, right? Do we need to worry about this old buddy of yours?"

He kept his tone even and firm.

"Like I already told you, Donald owes me. He knows I have more on him than he could ever get on me."

"Then the only thing left is to *kill the kid*," his partner had said before hanging up.

He looked over at the child now, trying to calculate how much longer before he had to do it. If he and his partner left Tuesday, he'd need to act soon so he had time to bury the body securely—some place deep in the forest.

Then he looked around the cottage, thinking what a good idea it had been to use the place, but remembering a happier time, many years ago, when he'd first come here to hide. He'd spent a few years of the only bliss he'd ever known in this deserted, quiet spot, planning a different kind of future. How immature and full of hope he'd been!

Maybe that was what made him hesitate. This place dredged up memories that he'd long since tried to bury—a period in his life before cheating and stealing and killing had begun. A time before danger finally caught up with him, slapped him in the face, and then taught him how to survive in the real world.

He knew this young one was just another meal ticket; he had to act to ensure that ticket didn't become a liability. The authorities were on alert; the child's picture was all over the papers and news. And even though his partner had never before asked him to kill someone, they both knew it had to be done. The little one could identify their faces.

He stood and walked to the window, staring out at the glistening lake, thinking about how to accomplish the task. Shooting would be quick and effective, but the vision of red stickiness against blond curls kept popping into his head. It didn't feel right.

Suddenly, he knew what he had to do. He picked the child up gently and carried the snoozing form down the wooded path to the lake, laying the small body gently on the ground, then bending over and taking off his shoes. The sand felt warm on his feet. Did that mean the water would be warm? He hoped so, though he didn't understand his own thinking.

He shook himself, then scooped the child up close to his chest and slowly walked into the lake until the water was at his waist. When it got to his upper chest, he lifted the body high above his head. The child stirred; eyelids flickered opened and he was staring into eyes so deep blue they looked purple.

He flung his burden as far as he could.

CHAPTER ONE

MAGGIE TURNER SHUT THE front door quietly and returned to the living room. She bent to the coffee table and picked up three empty coffee mugs, carrying them into the kitchen. Rinsing them out, she placed them in the dishwasher, and then stood for a moment, gazing out the window and waiting. She was cold, and her neck ached from holding her body so erect. She would have liked to return to her bed, pull up the covers and cease feeling. But she wouldn't; she couldn't.

Instead, she waited for the next knock on her door, knowing her neighbor, Dottie Alstead, would be over. Somehow, Dottie always knew when company arrived at Maggie's house

—especially when that company was someone as interesting as the police.

The officers had tried to be kind; Maggie knew that. They were new on the force and treated her like all the others had at first—like a piece of delicate glass, ready to shatter at the slightest touch. Then wondered why she didn't.

They did not understand that her sorrow lay too deep; her years of waiting for something to happen were too long. Maggie had done a lot of falling apart at first, but she'd gotten beyond that stage.

The knock on the kitchen door came, and Maggie turned from the sink to let her neighbor in.

"Oh, Maggie," Dottie gushed. Dottie rarely talked without some gushing.

"Was that the police? Did they have some word about Jenna?"

"Nothing significant—a few more sightings that will probably go nowhere. A few more questions based on the sightings," Maggie answered. She sat down at the kitchen table, her knees no longer able support her stiff posture.

"Then why do you look so pale?" Dottie asked, peering closely into Maggie's face.

Maggie turned her face toward the petite, blond woman, who despite her forty-plus years, dressed like a teenager. Today, Dottie wore a tube top and short, cut-off jeans that would have looked much better on someone who had curves.

I wish she'd keep her nose out of all this, Maggie thought for the hundredth time. She knew it was an unproductive thought.

For some reason, Dottie considered Maggie a close friend even though all they had in common was proximity and the fact they went to the same high school.

Well, that, and maybe the fact she adores Chad. At least I got over that phase of my life, Maggie thought.

Dottie was one of a handful of girls from their hometown of Lancaster, Pennsylvania, who seemed to still have a crush on Maggie's ex-husband, the star of the high school football team.

Maggie sighed, knowing that if she didn't come up with something more to say, Dottie would simply keep prying. Her neighbor fed off sensationalism, and she'd hit the jackpot when Maggie's girl went missing.

Maggie might as well tell her about the police visit.

"They are investigating a similar kidnapping that took place in Allentown. A little boy taken from a mall store in the middle of the day. An Amber alert went out yesterday, and I guess they're looking into possible connections."

"Oh, Maggie," cried Dottie, fat tears welling in her eyes. Unlike Maggie, Dottie didn't need much of a reason to cry.

"How very painful this must be! To dredge up all those memories."

Dottie reached across the kitchen table to grab Maggie's arm. Maggie simply glanced at the hand now clasping her forearm, and then glanced longingly at the kitchen door. Should she just ask her neighbor to please leave?

Dottie's clicking tongue cut through her thoughts, reminding Maggie how difficult it was to avoid her neighbor's advice. "And just when things were starting to settle down for you. Maybe this will lead to something," Dottie said.

She sat back, as if to give the moment an appropriate pause before continuing.

"Maybe if the two cases are linked, you can find out what happened to Jenna and get some closure."

Maggie felt a prickle of annoyance. As usual, Dottie was oblivious to the fact Maggie didn't want to hear those words. Dottie grasped her own throat with one of her pink-manicured hands.

"Does this mean they're reopening Jenna's case?" she asked in a raspy whisper.

The question extinguished Maggie's irritability and replaced it with exhaustion. She sighed deeply.

"No, I don't believe so. In fact, the officers who came today kept referring to Jenna in the past tense. I believe they are convinced she's long dead."

Dottie was nodding, not hearing what Maggie said, but skipping ahead to her next conclusion.

"Maybe this kind of closure is just what you need to get on with your life. Maybe you and your husband can get back together and work on your relationship; have another child..."

Maggie's anger was back.

"I believe I've told you, Dottie," she said slowly. "Chad and I are not together anymore and never will be. Even *when* I get my Jenna back."

But she dropped her head to her chest to get her emotions in check. Taking her frustrations out on her neighbor would accomplish nothing. When she lifted her head again, she could see Dottie's distaste—how dare Maggie speak out against the great Chad Turner! Suddenly Maggie could take no more.

"If you don't mind, I would like to be alone for a while to contemplate this...closure."

"Of course, dear," her neighbor chirped, happy to leave now that she'd tossed out the day's tidbit of advice.

Maggie returned to the living room and sat down in her favorite chair, her knees wobbly. The officers had shaken Maggie with news of another missing child. Could the two cases be related? Their arrival had reminded her also that the police had given up on her child many months ago.

Then her neighbor's mention of Chad had triggered painful memories of her failed marriage and the awful years before her daughter was taken and the even-more-awful years right afterwards.

Jenna. Her beautiful daughter, who'd abolished any pain of that bad marriage by creating the need only to be a mom—a mom who even today could feel the presence of her daughter. Maggie rose and wandered down the hall as she had many times, coming to an open door. The room was painted yellow with a wide strip of wallpaper decorated with Noah's ark figures. The theme was carried through with figurines on shelves and pillow accents. Though the baby crib was long gone,—Jenna was four when she disappeared—her little girl had loved the story of animals boarding a ship two by two. Even though the theme had been chosen when Jenna was an infant, Maggie hadn't replaced the theme with the more girly things she knew Jenna would want eventually. *Would she ever get the chance now?*

Maggie closed the door to Jenna's room and went back to her chair in the living room.

She sat back and let the feeling of Jenna wash over her. She didn't care anymore that others thought she was nuts for feeling this connection. She could see in the eyes of the few friends she still socialized with that, like the police, they all believed her child was dead and that Maggie had gone off the deep end in her constant efforts to find new ways to search.

It had taken a year of pure grief, followed by a year of getting back to work to get her head on straight, and during all of that time, she continued to work towards one goal: having the strength and the financial resources to pursue what she knew was true.

Jenna is alive. I would know if she wasn't. I feel her presence. She's out there somewhere, waiting for me to find her.

She went to her desk, sat down, and brought up Google. But she had no name to type.

What was the name of the detective? What was it?

She tilted her head, letting her mind return to a day last week when she'd met the young girl in the wheelchair at the doctor's office. The girl held an adorable toddler on her lap who was sniffling as much as Maggie. The two women had struck up a friendly conversation.

The pretty young woman explained that the baby had been a miracle—the woman had been paralyzed in her early teens, fallen in love at age twenty and had a son a year and a half later.

Maggie had cooed over the lively, robust "August," as the baby was named, and smiled when the young mother explained that they'd chosen the name August Samuel Jones, even though it was a mouthful, to honor her husband Danny's mentor "Gus" as well as Samuel. Samuel was a detective who had helped the couple with a criminal case, then hired the woman in the wheelchair to help in his office. The young woman had gone on and on about how great her boss was and how talented he was at solving difficult puzzles.

But had the mother mentioned a last name for Samuel?

Maggie rubbed her temples with both hands, the detective's full name on the edge of her consciousness—something that began with an O.

She dropped her hands, picked up the phone book, and turned to the yellow pages to look under "security" and the "O's".

A small ad was nestled among the listings.

"Here he is," Maggie whispered. "Samuel Osborne, private investigator. No job too small or too big."

CHAPTER TWO

SAM HUNG HIS COAT on the rack inside the door, waved at his assistant, Casey Jones, then went into his personal office. He sat down at the only piece of furniture he hadn't discarded on his last move—an office desk. The desk, which Sam had used for more than a decade on the police force, had been presented to him as a departure gift. It reminded him how much he'd enjoyed his time on the force.

"Everything okay this morning, Sam?" Casey asked, her green eyes sparkling. She'd wheeled after him into his office and deposited yesterday's mail on the desk.

Sam drank in her cheerfulness and thanked his lucky stars, as he did every day, for Casey's pretty blond presence as well as her sharp mind. Sam had stopped seeing the wheelchair a long time ago.

He was gradually giving her more and more of the investigative follow-up. Casey had been with him now for several years, starting as a part-timer as she sought a business degree and her husband pursued law enforcement. When she'd married Danny, who was now a full-time policeman, Sam had been part of the wedding party. Casey, Danny, and their little boy Gus had become Sam's family.

"Everything's fine," Sam answered, smiling and leaning over to take the mail.

"I've tied up the loose ends on our last case," he continued.

He sat back in his desk chair then, a sheep-ish grin on his face.

"I must say, Casey, after having you and Danny fall in love while I was investigating your case, then helping Rosie and Jacob solve their problem and watching them gravitate to-wards romance, I feel like some kind of Cupid. Love seems to follow me around..."

Casey chuckled softly. A look at the note-book on her lap, however, brought her merri-ment to a halt.

"Well, I don't think that *magic* will apply to your next job."

Sam looked up from the mail.

"You have an appointment with Margaret Turner for a new case tomorrow afternoon at 1 o'clock."

Sam cocked his head.

"Why is that name familiar?"

"A couple of years back, her daughter was kidnapped. She paid the ransom and the police and FBI launched an investigation, but never located the child."

The smile disappeared from Sam's face.

"I remember now. What does she think I can do for her that the Lancaster police or the FBI couldn't?"

"I don't know, Sam. She sounded pretty desperate and insistent. I guess the police came to her house and questioned her in relation to the kidnapping in Allentown a couple days ago. She doesn't know if there is any connection, but she insists her daughter is still out there and that police have given up on her daughter's case."

He was frowning now. "I can't help her," he said firmly. "I'm not the man for her case." His eyes returned to his mail, his manner now brusque.

Casey's expression softened. She'd known that Sam would resist, and she knew he was not being rude to her. She maneuvered her chair closer and dropped a file on the desk.

"I think she's looking to pursue new angles. If anyone can solve this case, it's you, Sam. But whether you take it or not, you can be the one to tell her 'no.' She'll be here tomorrow at one."

She turned her wheelchair away and left.

Within the hour, Sam walked out of his inner office to deposit the file back on Casey's desk.

"Think I'll go upstairs and grab a bite," he said, his smile back on his face. "See you in an hour or so."

As he climbed upstairs to his living quarters, thoughts of the kidnapping and what he'd read in those files, as well as what he'd seen in the papers about the Allentown case, hit him hard, and he muttered to himself.

"I can't do it. I just can't do a kidnapping."

He was still muttering as he fixed a sandwich and sat in his favorite chair. The sandwich was left untouched. Sam pushed his chair back, sandwich and plate still on his lap and closed his eyes.

It had been fourteen years since his son, Davie, had disappeared. Despite the fevered investigation he launched, Sam had never found his son. Meanwhile, the hunt had cost him his job and contributed to his divorce. His wife blamed him for their loss; he blamed himself, too. His father's death left him even emptier, but the resulting inheritance had given him a direction: private investigation. Solving cases gave him peace from his past.

Tears filled Sam's eyes.

I've worked too long at putting my life back together. How can I avoid the darkness if I work on a kidnapping case?

CHAPTER THREE

SAM DIDN'T SLEEP WELL that night. He tossed and turned, his mind never leaving the pain of his past for long.

Although he'd kept his brain preoccupied that morning with more research on the Jenna Turner and Allentown cases, he told himself it was just a diversion. It was disturbing reading: both children simply disappeared without a trace while shopping with parents at clothing stores. Sam had lost his own son at a store, though it hadn't been a clothing store.

Not much else had been written yet about the Allentown case, which happened two days ago. The parents were just now appealing to the public for help, but few details had been given except for a description of the boy and where he'd gone missing.

In the Turner case, old news reports talked about how the police came late to the case—just a few hours before the ransom drop, and the FBI even later—after the drop had occurred. A number of officers combed the area where the girl was taken as well as where the ransom drop had been staged, but they came up with no clues reported in the news, no leads, eye witnesses or even any viable suspects—a puzzle that paralleled what had happened in his own life. Sam was too close to that pain to think clearly and without emotion, as a good investigator should, and he knew it.

As the hour of one drew nigh, he grew more and more agitated. He had to find a kind way to refuse the case. He had already put together a list of associates that might consider taking it, if Ms. Turner had enough money and the drive to push forward.

When Maggie Turner walked into his office, Sam knew almost immediately how difficult turning her down was going to be. It wasn't that she was beautiful, though her soft wheat-colored hair topped a body that somehow managed to look both athletic and ripe.

It was her eyes. When she sat down and placed her folded hands on her lap, she looked up from those hands, and Sam felt a jolt. Her eyes were a royal, rich violet—an unusual color he couldn't remember ever seeing before. They held hope and desperation—a strange combination Sam remembered from the early days of his own son's kidnapping and the investigation. From his experience, he knew that hope was all that was keeping her going. No matter how futile the situation was, she believed Sam could help or she wouldn't be here.

"Thank you for seeing me," she said in a tired voice tinged with sadness. Although her brow was crinkled with worry lines, Sam could see no signs of permanent laugh wrinkles around those large eyes or her small, perfect mouth.

She looks like she's in her thirties, not forties, Sam thought.

"I know how good an investigator you are. I already called and talked to several of your clients. I also know the police believe my child is dead."

The tired voice was replaced by steel.

"But I do not. Are you familiar with my case?"

"I spent the morning reading up on it, as well as the kidnapping in Allentown this week," Sam said. "And I called my police connections for additional insight. So yes, I know a bit of what the police know," Sam said softly.

Instead of launching into a rehash or giving additional details, Maggie said simply, "Do you think Jenna's dead because it's been so long?"

Sam's eyes widened. What did she expect him to say?

"Probably." Sam desperately wanted to lie but he knew she needed to face the possibilities.

She did not crumble, get angry, or disgusted. She sat looking at Sam, her violet eyes penetrating his skull.

"She isn't," was all she said.

"And you know this how?" Sam couldn't help asking.

"Because I feel her. I talk to her every day, and I feel her talking back to me. I know that sounds crazy—she was only four when she was taken and now, she's just over six. But she's safe; she's well. She isn't being hurt."

Sam just sat in silence, not knowing how to react.

Maggie sighed deeply. Her head bowed for a moment as if she were gathering the strength to go on. When her head came up, Sam saw determination.

"Look. I don't care what you believe you know. I don't care what the statistics or the police say. I want to hire a professional who has more time than the police to look into what happened. Someone who might think differently from how they've been trained to think in the usual kidnapping cases."

Sam was nodding his head, still trying to come up with a kind way to say 'no.'

"I can pay you, Mr. Osborne. I renewed my real estate license last year, and though the housing market is still a little tough, I've made some sales. I've saved every penny of every commission I've made in the last six months—"

She stopped when Sam held up his hand, palm outward.

"Money is not the issue here, Ms. Turner. As you probably already know if you've researched who I am, an inheritance left me the luxury of taking only the cases I want to take."

He saw doubt creep into her face then, but the fire did not go out of her eyes.

"Mr. Osborne, I know that in Jenna's case, the police think they did what they could, but all of it never quite added up. The ransom was not that high, Jenna was taken right out from under my nose, the kidnappers let me talk to her that very afternoon, and she didn't sound scared or harmed. But then... she just disappeared out of my life! No second demands, no clues, nothing except a few crack pot sightings."

Sam scratched his head. He'd thought much the same thing when he'd gone through the notes. He knew that even though Maggie herself was not a rich woman, she came from a fairly wealthy family. She might well have been able to raise more than the $250,000 demanded if the kidnappers had allowed more time.

"Ms. Turner, is it okay to call you by your first name? Margaret, is it? And please call me Sam. Look, I'm not saying I'll take this case, but let's start at the beginning. I know you've told this a million times, but go over for me how she was taken."

Hope replaced the doubt in Maggie's eyes, and Sam swallowed and turned away. He picked up a notebook as much to give his hands something to do as to take notes.

"First name? Of course, but I'm no Margaret. Call me Maggie." She cleared her throat and began.

"Jenna and I spent the afternoon shopping in a store we frequented regularly because it carries both little girl clothes and ladies' fashions."

Her face relaxed as she pulled out a pleasant memory and almost smiled.

"Even though she was just four, she was already quite the shopper. She loved to help me pick out clothes as much as she loved to pick out her own.

"We'd already chosen a new Easter dress for her, so we were looking for something for me. Jenna loved to play hide and seek behind the dresses. Because we've been in the store so much, the clerks knew it and usually played along." Maggie studied the back of one hand, before raising it to her mouth and taking a small swipe. Her eyes connected with Sam's again.

"Jenna was full of giggles and having so much fun. I was not paying attention to her like I should have been. My mind was on whether I had the time or the desire to try one of the dresses on. I decided it was getting late, so I took one I was considering off the rack and was headed to the dressing room. I turned back to get Jenna. I couldn't see her, so I called her name."

Now Maggie's face took on the same pan-icked look she must have worn two-and-a-half years ago when she discovered her daughter missing.

"The clerk, store owner, and I searched and searched—every rack, every dressing room. When it hit me that this wasn't a game, I'm afraid I let out an awful scream."

Maggie use the palm of the same hand to swipe her entire face, then refolded her hands together in her lap.

"I don't remember much about what hap-pened during the next few hours—it's all a blur, talking to the security guard and eventually the police. Question after question… I went home finally, when the searching ended at the mall. The ransom demand came shortly after that. We arranged for the money, and I made the ransom drop early that evening. The FBI arrived just minutes after the drop and my return home. But I'm afraid it was too late by then. My Jenna was truly gone somewhere…"

Her eyes looked haunted and tragic.

Sam knew from experience that the next stage of this conversation would be self-recrimination, which would do neither of them any good.

To bring her back to the present, he interrupted.

"How well did you know the store owner?"

Maggie's thoughts returned to the room and the present conversation.

"Jenna and I had been in this store dozens of times, and I usually dealt directly with the owner, Francine. I've been going to the store for many years, so I know her pretty well—the clerk that worked there not so well."

She tilted her head.

"I don't know why either would have anything to do with it. I know the police and the FBI extensively questioned Francine and her clerk, as well as another clerk, right after the incident. Francine even appeared on one of the news reports with me, making the same appeals I did."

"I'm not really suggesting the store had anything to do with it, I'm just getting some initial facts," Sam said. He scribbled as he talked.

"Tell me about what authorities did and about this ransom."

Maggie sat back in her chair.

"The money my husband and I had on hand went to pay the ransom. We only had a few hours, so we cashed in some CDs and stock, and borrowed a chunk from my father until we could get more. To pay my father back, we eventually put our house on the market."

She looked up at Sam again, pain evident in the expression.

"I hated the thought of selling the house. I kept thinking… what if Jenna should find her way home and I'm not there? Luckily, my father insisted on buying the house himself, and he lets us… well me, now…rent it," she added. "And I've been paying Dad the money we owe gradually."

Sam glanced up at Maggie in time to see a small shudder. She wrapped her arms around her as if she were cold.

Sam said softly, "We do what we have to do—and then pray that it's the right thing."

The two sat in silence for a few moments, not saying a word. They seemed to become aware of the quiet at the same time and suddenly looked uncomfortable.

Maggie sighed and continued.

"The call came only a few hours after the kidnapping. I talked to Jenna for just a few moments, and then someone got on the line and told us to put the money into a bag they'd left on our front porch sometime while we were at the store. The kidnappers told us to take the money to Miller Park, put it in a specific barrel beside the third bench from the entrance on Pine Street. We were warned, of course, that if there was police involvement, the deal was off and Jenna would be killed."

"You called the police anyway?"

Maggie's brow furrowed.

"Chad fought me on that one, but I made the decision to involve the police. I called them on my way home from the store. The kidnappers' call at home got to me before police arrived. It was just an hour or so before the drop off. At the park, police were about as inconspicuous as you can be. I swear I was looking for them myself the whole time I was in the park, and I never spotted anyone who gave themselves away... but..."

She didn't need to say more, as Sam knew her loss for words was a silent, *obviously it didn't work.*

"Chad was furious with me for contacting

the police, but I really believed it was the right thing to do."

"You did what you thought was right," Sam tried to reassure her, but he watched as one tear slid down her face and landed in her lap. She wiped it away impatiently and straightened her shoulders.

"I put the bag with the money in the barrel just as I was told and walked back to the entrance of the park as instructed. A young man on a bicycle passed me and entered the park. Police say he stopped at that barrel, picked up a bag, and biked to the other side of the park. By the time they took him down, I was running towards the action, anxious to find out something—*anything*. The guy on the ground tackled by the police was holding an empty bag. He confessed later that a man paid him $50 just a few minutes earlier to pick the bag up. His story checked out both with police, and later with the FBI."

"The boy knew nothing; the money was not in that bag. Jenna was gone. We waited for days at home, expecting, hoping to hear where she was, demand for more money. Anything. No one called. Nothing happened. The FBI came, the news cameras arrived and, well, you know the rest. It took several weeks before Jenna's disappearance was old news."

Maggie's head was now bowed, her hands resting in her lap, her shoulders drooping. She was reliving the despair of the wait, just as Sam had lived it.

What was he going to do? How could he possibly help someone when he hadn't been able to help himself?

When Maggie was again in control, she lifted her head, her gaze now steady. Those shocking eyes were full of question; Sam already knew he was going to get involved.

"Yes, Maggie. I'll help you find her."

CHAPTER FOUR

SAM KNEW HE NEEDED to start by getting more info from the Lancaster police. Fortunately, he had an unusually good relationship with the local force through his connection to Casey's husband and through Captain Robert McCoy, a close friend of many years. Bob and Sam had served together on the Philadelphia police force. Sam also had a reputation with local authorities for cooperation and had helped police with several cases. They, in turn, were more than willing to give him the background he often needed.

Sam knew the local police enough to know they'd done everything by the books. As Maggie had explained, the FBI hadn't gotten involved until after the ransom drop; there hadn't been time.

Sam also knew, however, how limited the resources of the local force were and how difficult it was to pick up a scent for any law enforcement after the crime had been committed.

"Sam, how delightful to see you," Bob McCoy said, as he reached over to shake Sam's hand.

"It's been way too long, Bob. We're overdue for a beer and a burger, if Melissa will let you indulge. How is she, anyway? And how are the grandkids?"

"I'm not sure who drives me crazier, Sam. But both my loving wife and my children's off-spring are doing just fine. Little Stevie started kindergarten this year, if you can believe that—the last one to go off to school. Sit down, Sam, we'll get caught up after we talk business. Coffee?" Bob asked.

Sam smiled and sat.

"No, thanks, Bob. I treasure my stomach too much for that. I remember what your coffee tastes like."

"Well, then, what can I do for you?

Sam decided to launch right into it. Bob wouldn't fall for tiptoeing around a subject.

"I've been hired to work on the Turner

kidnapping," he said. Bob looked surprised, then sat back in his chair and put his hands behind his head.

"That's pretty much a lost cause from our angle now, my friend," he said. "We've done our investigation, followed every lead we could find and run up against a brick wall. I guess I shouldn't be surprised Mrs. Turner hired you; she's desperate for some news. I thought you didn't take kidnapping cases though. Why the hell would you put yourself through this?"

He sat forward then, put his elbows against his desk and fisted his hands together.

"What are you hoping to accomplish?"

Sam didn't answer for a minute.

"I'm not sure, Bob. I'm not sure I can find anything, but maybe I just need to look. The woman got to me. She's as convinced that her daughter is alive as I am that Davie is out there somewhere. And then this kidnapping happened in Allentown, and I just want to rule out the possibility the two aren't connected."

Bob shook his head back and forth, and then made sure he had Sam's full attention before continuing.

"Look, Sam. In your case, there's a chance someone took your son just because they wanted a kid. You never heard a word. But in the Turner case? Not likely. They asked for a ransom and got it. The girl never surfaced. You know as well as I do once a ransom has been paid and the child is not returned, the kidnappers have made the decision to get rid of the witness. I'm afraid the FBI agents I worked with agreed."

Despite the harsh assessment, Bob's forehead was wrinkled in concern. Sam knew it was as much because he'd taken the case as it was worry over the child's fate.

"I know," Sam replied. "I don't know why I agreed. I guess I'm going on my gut here. Maybe I need to feel like I'm trying to save Davie again by helping Maggie Turner out. Maybe enough years have passed that it's time for me to face my fears. I don't know what this is. I just know I've committed to trying. I could use any help you can give me."

"I'll do what I can legally do, Sam. And I should have some more information on Allentown if it comes through. But reviewing case files doesn't tell you that much. The Jenna Turner kidnappers were clever – they knew how to take advantage of a police department that had almost no experience with kidnapping. The FBI also treated us with scorn, Sam, even though it's not our fault they couldn't be brought into the picture until after the money was gone."

He took a sip of his coffee, a look of distaste replacing the worry lines.

"They weren't much help either, at least not locally. Even though there were many sightings after the missing child bulletin went out, most were false leads, which I guess is common in cases involving children. Everybody wants to help. The FBI pulled out physically pretty quickly, though I'm sure they did what they could with a cold trail."

"Since your officers were there at the drop, how do you think the kidnappers got away with the money?" Sam asked.

Bob just sat staring at his coffee cup.

"To start, the bag itself should have put up a red flag. I actually never heard of a kidnapper providing the bag. The Turners received a common satchel found in just about every Walmart or Kmart on their doorstep the very day the kidnapping occurred—we suspect it arrived about the same time as the actual snatching."

He looked up at Sam then.

"Mrs. Turner had to come up with cash within hours of being contacted. She was told to put the money in the trashcan and walk away as instructed. A rider came by and 're-trieved' it. What he really did was pick up a bag the kidnapper already put in a trashcan. There were two cans attached side by side and the one he picked up was probably from the second can. The hired bicyclist was told to look under the top papers of the right can for a bag with a string. It still had the string when we picked him up.

"By the time the tracer we put on the real bag with the money was run, the cash was long gone, the true bag abandoned in an alley. The kidnappers were probably laughing their asses off, watching while we chased the bicyclist. We managed to keep that aspect of this case out of the news, but I'm afraid it wasn't our finest hour."

He shook his head slowly.

Sam nodded his head in agreement. "You didn't have very much time to plan a response, Bob. I know you can't just hand me the case files, and I know the FBI did some of the follow up, but can you give me some basics to start? I realize I'll be covering some of the same ground, but I want to take this from a fresh perspective, maybe expand outward from the people you talked to."

"Sam, you know I'll give you what I can." Bob stood. "But you owe me that burger. Let's do this week if we can. I'll have a preliminary list of facts for you and anything I find out about Allentown. I expect you, as always, to keep us appraised of anything you find out."

Sam rose in turn, knowing what a busy schedule his friend had. He smiled broadly and reached for his hand.

"It would be my honor, Captain."

CHAPTER FIVE

"ARE YOU COMPLETELY CRAZY?" Chad Turner stood, his face red, his voice in an almost-scream. His fist was in Maggie's face, but she knew he wouldn't strike her. His weapons had always been words and threats.

"I cannot just give up," she said calmly. "And I don't understand how you can. I know Jenna is still alive."

"And just how do you intend to pay for a private detective?" Chad shouted. "You sucked us dry, Maggie, between the ransom and the psychics and the consultants that first year. It's taken me this long to recover. Why in the hell would you start this up again?"

His fist had come down and he was pacing,

his hands behind his back. He turned to glare at her, an expression she was used to by now.

"Even if we had the money, you need to face the facts. Maybe instead of padding the pockets of some hotshot investigator, you need to spend that money on a shrink. Talk to someone about how you broke this marriage while you were breaking your own heart over the tragedy of Jenna."

Maggie's eyes turned cold as she looked at this man she used to love. She knew better than Chad that the marriage never really got off the ground. Trauma and differing views on what to do about Jenna had pushed that marriage out the exit and slammed the door. The fact that Chad was having an affair with a co-worker when divorce finally came up was not a surprise to Maggie.

She didn't really understand, however, how Chad could give up on Jenna. After their daughter's birth, he had been a doting father, proud of producing an offspring and enjoying the novelty of fatherhood. He'd left ninety percent of the parenting up to Maggie, including most of the day-to-day care. But he'd clearly enjoyed the ten percent, which included much gift giving to make up for his frequent absence.

Now, Chad couldn't seem to understand why Maggie didn't just "get on with her life," as he had, moving out of the home they'd shared and marrying the co-worker who'd caught his eye.

Maggie straightened her shoulders.

"I made commission on three houses this year, Chad. The realty agency says that's pretty incredible in a market in recovery. Sam Osborne hasn't told me exactly how much it will be, but I've got a good start on the funds I'll need. I just thought you might want to help. I've never asked you for much."

Chad sighed and finally sat down on a stiff-backed kitchen chair. He rubbed one hand over his face, and then looked up at Maggie.

"I have a new life, Maggie. A new woman who loves me more than you ever did. We're looking for a house. We want to have a baby…"

The steel in Maggie's eyes sparked.

"A baby. A *baby*. Your baby is out there needing your help!" she said with disgust.

Chad rose slowly from the chair and turned to face Maggie.

"Well, guess what. I don't agree, and I'm not spending another nickel on this wild goose chase. If that fool detective will work for the few pennies you have, then he can't be very good. And he will not get support from me. Jenna is dead. Accept that reality and get on with your life."

Chad turned away from her and hurried towards his new car. Maggie just stood shivering despite the heat of the day, watching the shiny sports car peal out of the driveway and speed off.

I can't believe I married such a narcissist. She turned and went back inside.

Chad paid no attention to speed limits as he found his way to Sam's office/home address. He pulled his fancy new car to the curb, slammed the car door and almost ran up the sidewalk, threw the front door open and blundered inside, prepared for battle.

Casey looked up at a red-faced man standing at the edge of her desk.

"Where is that son of a bitch?" Chad screamed.

Sam heard Chad even with his office door shut. He rose from behind his desk, carried a baseball bat he always kept under his desk and set it carefully inside the office door before stepping outside into the outer office.

"What seems to be the problem?" he asked the man standing at Casey's desk breathing heavily. Sam recognized Chad Turner from television and pictures in his file, but the farm boy, all-American face was contorted with rage.

"How dare you con my wife!" Chad huffed at Sam, once again shaking a fist. "You won't get a cent out of me – not one red cent. Maggie has very little money of her own, *do you understand?* What little we had as a couple went first to the ransom, and then to the so-called experts Maggie has already paid. They all promised to find Jenna. But she's dead. You know that. I know that. We all know it!"

"Then perhaps you have information the police and the FBI do not have," Sam said quietly. "Would you like to share your theories and information with me in my office here?"

He gestured to his open office door.

"Maggie has paid a small retaining fee. So I'm already on the clock."

Chad's transformation was immediate. He breathed in, then out slowly while his face reflected confusion, then suspicion. He stood shifting from foot to foot, thinking. When Sam walked to the inner office, Chad followed. Sam smiled reassurance at Casey, and then shut the door.

When both men were seated, Sam asked quietly, "Well, what do you know that the rest of us don't?"

"I just know it's crazy for Maggie to hire someone to beat a dead horse. It's been two-and-a-half years, Mr. Osborne. Maggie has talked to psychics and so-called 'finders' and all kinds of kidnapping experts. She called the police constantly with false leads these experts provided. She's convinced herself she's connected through some spiritual thread to our poor dead child."

He studied his hands before looking up at Sam.

"I just refuse to spend another cent on something I'm certain is foolish, Mr. Osborne. And I'm tired of seeing Maggie beat herself up over this. She needs to accept reality."

"It's considerate of you to try and help Maggie 'accept reality,' Mr. Turner. But she has to want to do that. She's convinced I can give a fresh perspective on the case. I would not have taken her retainer if I didn't agree. She came to me in control of her senses, and I have no intention of bleeding her dry. If there's even a minute chance your daughter is alive, I will work to find her. I gave my word to your ex-wife, and I always keep my word."

Chad leaned forward then and put both palms flat on Sam's desk. He glared into the detective's face.

"Well, you're as much of a damn fool as she is, then." Chad pushed himself into a stand and turned, slamming first Sam's office door, then the door to the outside as he left.

Sam followed him out into the outer office, and then turned to smile at Casey.

"Quite a blowhard, isn't he?" he said before

returning to his desk. Once seated, he leaned back to study the ceiling.

Well, I still have doubts about taking this case. But I think this jerk just pushed me over the edge.

CHAPTER SIX

THE CHILD CAME UP splashing and laughing. The man dove in and connected with feet, then scooped the small body up.

"I like to swim, but the water is awfully cold. Can we do it another time?" the giggling youngster said.

He raised the child up in his arms and headed for shore.

Enough. I've just had enough, the man thought.

Back at the cabin, he set the skinny body down on an old armchair and found a blanket.

The child pulled the blanket closer and laid back against the back of the chair. Round eyes reflected no fear, but the playfulness was gone.

Only weariness remained. "I think I would like to go home now. Mommy will be worried."

"Your mother knows where you are, little one. She can't keep you with her right now, so she gave you to me to keep you safe."

"No," the small voice replied. "Mommy wouldn't do that."

He got up to stoke the fire. "I know you love your mommy. But she's in great danger from the people who are after you. She told me to find you a good home to stay for now," he said, pausing with the poker in his hand.

"Will you protect me then?" the child asked.

"I can't keep you, but I'll get you a nice place to live."

"I want to go home," the little one insisted, and for the first time in the last three days, tears began to fall.

"Shush, now. Here's your milk. Go to sleep, little one. Let me think for a while."

After a few sips and several minutes, the child's eyes closed, the small chest began its steady up and down rhythm.

And the man began to pace.

"What can I do? What are my options?" he whispered to the cabin walls.

The fire burned low for hours. Several times, he got up to put another log on the stack and return to his chair. Finally, he climbed a rickety, old ladder to a tiny attic, opened a high backed dresser and took out several items. A well-worn brown felt hat, a stiff pair of old fashioned britches, a tackle box and a leather Bible, which he looked at with distaste. He laid the clothes and box on the floor, and carried the Bible with him down the ladder, a plan beginning to form in his mind.

CHAPTER SEVEN

AFTER GOING OVER THE notes Casey provided and notes from his conversation with police for the second time, Sam made a list of people to interview. Although police had talked to the Turners' neighbors, he decided to start with a canvas of the area where the family lived to see if anyone saw anything suspicious leading up to the disappearance. Investigators had said all the neighbors were accounted for at the time of the kidnapping and focused more heavily on the area where the little girl had been snatched.

First up on Sam's list were the neighbors across the street from Maggie Turner's home: Selma and Daryl Stewart.

The heavy front door of the Stewart home

was open, and Sam could hear voices through the screen door as he came up the walk. They seemed to be in the midst of an argument.

"You know we can't bring her here!" screamed a man's voice.

"I know that! But what's the point if we can't be with her? Why don't we move someplace where no one would know us? I can't stand being away from her."

"Maybe later," the man's voice said.

"Promise me," the woman said.

"I promise," the man said just before Sam rang the doorbell.

The argument seemed to have dissipated completely by the time a tall, slim woman with salt-and-pepper hair answered the door. Selma Stewart smiled warmly, as she ushered Sam in and showed him into a living room. Daryl rose from his seat on the sofa to shake Sam's hand, and then sat back down. Selma sat beside him.

"So, Maggie has hired a private eye," Daryl said. "Good for her. But what do you need from us? We talked to the police and FBI several times after Jenna disappeared."

"Mrs. Turner is convinced her daughter is still alive. I agreed to investigate and take a look at the situation from a different angle than police."

Sam flipped through his notes.

"I understand you reported a suspicious white van?" He looked from Daryl to Selma.

Selma Stewart frowned slightly.

"I called police myself. They always tell you to contact them if you think of something. At least, they do on television."

She practically huffed out the next words.

"But the police, and even the FBI, didn't seem to think it was significant."

She sat up straighter and tugged a sleeve into place.

"Then I guess this is a good place to begin," Sam said. He took out his notebook and flipped through a few pages.

"I'd like to hear about the van," Sam said.

Selma tugged at the other sleeve, then sat up a little straighter.

"I first noticed it about two weeks before the kidnapping. It was a very small white SUV; Daryl thought it was a Pathfinder. Anyway, it was parked every morning about three in front of 2226 Moran Way—we're at 2222— then left about 3 p.m. in the afternoon. It was never parked in the driveway, even though that driveway was empty most of the time. I just thought it was odd and pointed it out to Daryl at one point, and then to the authorities during questioning after the kidnapping. They told me it belonged to the man who was renting the house. He parked it out in the street because it leaked oil. Now, honestly, does that sound right?"

Daryl Stewart, a short, pudgy man with prominent ears and a balding head, smiled and patted his wife's hand. "I'm afraid, sir, that Selma sometimes gets overzealous when she latches onto an idea. We both felt a bit foolish when we learned why the van was parked on the street."

"Did he still park it in the street after the kidnapping?"

"No, not after the police talked to him. He parked it in the driveway for a day or two – then next thing we knew, it wasn't there at all. I think he moved out."

Selma harrumphed at the statement.

"That in itself is a bit mysterious, wouldn't you think? I don't think the man could have been living there more than a couple of months," she said.

Sam scribbled a few lines. "I wonder why it was there in the morning and disappeared at three every day. Do you know what he did for a living? Was he coming home from a job?" he asked.

"We never even saw him, except for a couple of times when I glanced out the window and he was going or coming close to 3 p.m. I am pretty sure one of the neighbors told me his name was Albert something-or-other."

"So this Albert sold the home?" Sam asked.

Selma shook her head.

"He was a renter. The home belongs to the Andersons. Betty couldn't sell it, or didn't want to, when Charles passed away. She was away in Europe visiting one of her kids that year. You could talk to the realtor who rented to the guy —she's helped a few of the neighbors rent out or sell their homes."

"Her name is Gretchen Myers," Daryl interjected. "And she's a real looker!" Sam looked up at him in time to see a wink.

"You would know," Selma, said, a look of mild disgust on her face.

Daryl patted her hand again. "Can't kill a man for just looking, Selma, dear."

Sam took down the name, and then asked a few questions about living across from the Turners. The Stewarts seemed to truly adore Jenna and expressed their pity for "the poor, lost Maggie" who they professed to be a good neighbor. They also mostly had positive things to say about Chad Turner, calling him friendly and full of amusing stories to tell at barbecues, though they said there hadn't been but a handful in their neighborhood in recent years. They also reported that Chad worked long hours and was rarely home.

As Selma and Daryl went on for a while about how traumatic the weeks after the kidnapping had been because of media hounds, Sam was making a note to have Casey track down possibilities for checking up on what he had heard as he walked up to the house. Who was it that "couldn't be brought here," Sam's curious brain questioned. He'd have Casey run a check on the Stewarts.

CHAPTER EIGHT

SAM HAD EVERY INTENTION of going to the next neighbor's house—Dorothy Alstead and turned toward the house after leaving the Stewarts.

When he looked over at Maggie's house, he saw her sitting on the porch swing, and his body switched direction. His feet headed to her house almost of their own volition.

"Hi," Maggie said, no surprise at seeing him in her voice or on her face. "I saw you go into the Stewarts and hoped you would stop by. Would you like some iced tea?"

"That sounds wonderful," he answered. "I could use a bit of throat soothing before I tackle your other next door neighbors."

"Sugar in your tea?" she asked.

"It probably would help my disposition, but no. I'm not fond of sweet tea."

She went inside to fetch refreshments. Sam sat down on one of the wrought iron chairs. He longed for a cigarette, and then was shocked by his inclination. It had been almost 15 years since he'd even lit one up. He sighed and sat back against the chair.

He wasn't sure why he'd stopped by.

Maggie came back with his iced tea, and then returned to her seat on the swing. They were both silent for a few minutes, enjoying the pleasant day, not sure what to say. Maggie smiled shyly, and Sam's mouth went to work.

"My ex-wife used to hate any pause in the conversation. I never quite figured out why. We were married almost ten years. I thought a few pauses in talking were deserved."

Maggie chuckled softly.

"I know what you mean. It was the same with Chad, especially in any social environment. God forbid that we have a dinner at a restaurant and not have a list of topics to cover. I think after a while, he gave up and just started doing all of the talking."

Sam chuckled with her, and then was silent again—lost in the depths of her huge, violet eyes.

So sad, but so full of intelligence, he thought.

Her voice cut through his reverie.

"What are you finding out?"

"I've just gotten started thinking about all this, Maggie, and one thing you already mentioned is bothering me. I know that $250,000 was a burden for you and Chad to scrape together, but like you said, it's a low amount for this kind of kidnapping. The criminals usually ask for a large amount, then sometimes settle when they find out the couple can't pay the millions. They also usually allow more time to scrape it together. Did you consider this kidnapping might be motivated by something other than just money?"

Maggie sipped her tea, then held it in her lap with both hands and cocked her head.

"You think money is not the reason someone took my Jenna?"

"It was well planned, so it was not a random kidnapping. Someone knew you'd be in that store. They knew how they could get away quickly. They knew you could scrape together some money quickly, but not millions."

"So they're good at what they do," Maggie said. "That's pretty obvious since the police couldn't find anything." A fat drop of moisture from the outside of her glass traveled its length and wet one of her fingers. She lifted her finger and licked it off, her thoughts on Sam's words.

The simple act brought Sam's eyes to her lips, and he noticed how pink they were. *What was wrong with him?* He didn't usually react physically to his own female clients, even the ones that were attractive. He looked down at his own glass before continuing.

"I think that whoever took Jenna had some idea of just how much you could come up with. Maybe they also had some other reason for picking your child."

"Is that good or bad? You think someone had it in for us?" Maggie asked him.

She really was quite lovely with her thick blond curls, slim body and those damn eyes. *Like Daryl Stewart said, you can't blame a guy for looking.* Sam took a sip of tea and let his professional side take over.

"It's a possibility, and one I don't think the police pursued. Can you think of anyone who has a grudge against you or your husband?"

"Ex-husband," she clarified. "And although I don't much care for him, most of the time, he comes across as charming and nice. I know he has a temper, but I don't think it has caused him any enemies—except maybe me."

She took a deep breath then posed her own question. "I guess that's a bit harsh. Can you understand that last statement since you were married?"

Sam chuckled again. "I understand completely. Our divorce wasn't exactly friendly, though I hold no major grudges against my wife. I also know that a tragedy like this one can take a big toll on any marriage – and especially if it isn't strong to begin with."

Maggie Turner was clearly surprised. "You sound experienced."

Sam wasn't ready to share his personal tragedy.

He stood and set the half-drunk glass of tea on a table.

"I know what it feels like to have a weak marriage and have it destroyed by events."

"Oh, of course. I'm sorry, Sam," Maggie said softly. She rose from the swing and set her own glass down, a look of concern on her face.

Sam smiled again to put her at ease. "Thanks for the tea, Maggie. It was very refreshing. I'd better get to work, though."

He turned and walked down three steps, then paused. He turned back around.

"It might be a good idea for us to get together later today to discuss some of my theories and what I find out. I think it will take most of this afternoon to handle what I need to do here in the neighborhood. Would you happen to be free for dinner?"

Maggie appeared to weigh her answer for a moment, but finally smiled in return.

"Yes. Sure. I'm certainly not busy today."

"See you at seven?" Sam asked.

"I look forward to it," she said.

Sam made sure Maggie did not see the grin on his face as he walked down the sidewalk and over to a neighbor's house.

CHAPTER NINE

"I WONDERED WHEN YOU'D be by to see me," Dottie gushed to Sam, a wide smile on her face. "You're that detective Maggie hired, aren't you?"

She gestured towards the interior of her house, and then began walking down the hall, talking as she went.

"As she probably told you, I'd do anything to help that poor woman. I'm practically her best friend in the world."

Sam's eyebrows lifted, though Dottie didn't see the action. Somehow he couldn't imagine this woman and Maggie as buddies.

Sam studied the bone-thin blond in a tight pair of jeans and a bright yellow shirt tied at the waist and unbuttoned at the top to reveal an equally tight undershirt and generous cleavage.

"I just put on a fresh pot of coffee," Dottie said. "May I offer you a cup?" she said.

"No, thank you... Mrs. Alstead is it?" Sam said, looking down at his notepad. "I do have some questions I need to ask."

Dottie filled a steaming mug and turned back to Sam.

"It's Dottie to anyone in this neighborhood, and that includes friends of the dear, pitiful Maggie. I feel so badly for her: I'm sure, like everyone, that her daughter is long dead. I just hope some pedophile didn't get hold of her first. I can't blame Maggie for trying to do something, however. Oh, forgive me, please sit down." She gestured to a kitchen chair and Sam sat.

Sam took a pen out of his shirt pocket and flipped the pages of the notebook.

"How long have you known the Turners?" he asked.

"Oh, forever—or so it seems. Maggie and I were classmates in school starting in elementary. Chad joined us during our freshman year of high school. They started dating their sophomore year of high school—a lovely couple. It's so tragic how they've been torn apart by this!

Poor Maggie is just nothing like she was in high school. And now she's lost Chad, as well as her girl."

Sam looked up from his notes. *Like Chad was such a prize*, he thought.

"How has she changed?"

Dottie sat and put her coffee mug on the table in front of her, leaning forward in her eagerness to share.

"In high school, I guess you'd say Maggie was one of the cool kids. She didn't have a lot of girlfriends because she kind of kept to herself, but the boys were clambering after her—at least before Chad came along. She's got that whole athletic, lean, graceful look about her, and then, her folks were well to do—her dad was president of First Third Bank here in town. She always had the best of clothes, the best of everything, even her own car. And the girls were jealous of her, especially after she snatched Chad up."

Dottie sipped her coffee, lost for a moment in her thoughts.

"Chad was popular, I take it?" Sam prodded.

Dottie's face took on a look of reverence as she stared out the kitchen window.

"Chad was the most handsome boy in school and the star of our football team. And since he came from out of town—I think it was just before high school that his family moved here—well, that made him all the more mysterious. From almost the beginning, though, he only had eyes for Maggie."

She sighed and returned to sipping coffee.

"Your neighbors, Selma and Daryl Stewart, told me about the white van parked on the street for a couple of weeks. Did you notice it, too?" Sam asked.

Dottie's attention returned to the room.

"Yea, I did. But I also saw the guy that lived in that house get into it and drive away in the afternoon a few times. I waved at him once or twice, but only got a nod. The guy just was not the neighborly type."

Dottie shivered slightly, then looked straight at Sam.

"Do you think he had something to do with all this?"

"I'm just looking into any unusual activity and Mrs. Stewart seemed to think it was odd he parked in the street," Sam replied. His head rose to meet Dottie's gaze.

"How well do you know the Stewarts?"

Dottie's eyebrows rose at the question. She set down her mug to think.

"Well, Selma can be a bit...enthusiastic about things. But they're nice enough, I guess. They've lived here quite a few years, but have never been really active in the neighborhood. Surely you don't think *they* had anything to do with this! I mean they argue quite a bit, even in public. And they were rejected for membership in the local country club, even though he's a big shot at the paper mill and they supposedly have scads of money. But kidnapping? I can't see what they'd have to gain."

Sam's eyes returned to his notebook. He could sense Dottie's intense focus on his face. When he looked back up, she tossed her blond hair and leaned back against the kitchen chair, jutting her chest forward and adjusting the collar of her shirt. She appeared to Sam to be absorbing new thoughts about the kidnapping and her neighborhood. Or maybe she was just wondering what else she could share with the detective. He decided to push a little further.

"Do you know of anyone with a grudge against Mr. or Mrs. Turner?"

Her eyes widened.

"You think maybe there was more to the kidnapping than just the ransom?"

"I don't have any thoughts on this case yet, Mrs. Alstead. Dottie. It's a standard question, and I thought since you're such good friends with Mrs. Turner and have known her so long…"

Dottie took a few minutes to think.

"No. Not really. I mean there were girls who didn't like her in high school, but that was so long ago."

"Anyone from those days then?" he prodded.

"Well, the Weaver twins did everything in their power to spread vicious rumors about Maggie, but no one paid them much mind. It was kind of their thing."

Dottie went on to describe the twins in detail—tall, blond and athletic like Maggie. She also shared a few stories about how athletic they were and what awards they won. *I guess she just admires the athletes*, Sam thought. He took a few notes.

"And Nancy Maddox always seemed to be trying to compete with Maggie, but she was an underclassman."

Sam wrote the additional name in his notebook. "Did Nancy Maddox have something against Maggie?" he said without looking up.

"No, not early on, anyway. She was two years younger than our class, and her family was wealthy like Maggie's. Nancy's dad was an officer at the same bank as Maggie's. When I say she was competitive, I'm referring to boys, not athletics like the twins. She seemed to go after the same boys as Maggie. Even tried to entice Chad away."

Sam looked up at her then.

She really has a thing for Maggie's ex, he thought.

Dottie rambled on. "In general, Nancy was kind of a bitch, really. Chad wasn't the only boyfriend she was after. Nobody really liked her, even before the big scandal."

Sam's eyebrows lifted.

"Scandal?"

"At the bank. Nancy's father got caught embezzling money – lots of money. He was sent to prison, and Nancy and her mother left town. I hadn't really even thought about the Maddox family in years. The scandal happened when we were seniors in high school."

Sam noted to have Casey check up on the embezzlement.

"And Chad? Did he have any enemies?"

Dottie straightened her collar again, and then used one hand to smooth her hair.

"Lots of boys were jealous of Chad in high school. Why wouldn't they be? He excelled at every sport there was. He was handsome, new to town. But since then? I guess I wouldn't know. I mean he's always very friendly the few times I've seen him. As you probably know, though, he hasn't been around much lately."

She tilted her head then.

"It's a shame, really. They were such a lovely couple. Maggie was so lucky to have snagged him—not just once, but twice. She moved away from Lancaster to Philly for a while. It was so romantic when she returned and then they got back together. Just like in high school…"

Sam looked up to see Dottie gazing out a window, lost in the high school days again. But he'd heard enough for now. He thanked his hostess and left.

CHAPTER TEN

MAGGIE WAS NERVOUS ABOUT going to dinner and couldn't understand why. It was true she hadn't been out much in the last few years—a few dinner dates with clients to discuss business, a few get-togethers with a handful of friends.

She shook her head and began rummaging in her closet, taking several items of clothing off hooks and throwing them on the bed.

How stupid is this. Sam is nice, but it's just a dinner invitation to discuss the case. I can certainly hold my own in a conversation.

With that comforting thought, she selected a bland-looking, but comfortable pant suit, tried it on, and then gazed into her full-length mirror.

I'm way too thin, and my skin is a mess. I'm going gray; I look like an old lady!

Maggie visualized the kind eyes of Sam and didn't want those eyes to see what she was seeing in the mirror. Sam didn't seem the type to care about fashion. The two times she'd seen him, he was dressed neatly in clothes that hugged his body and were well-made, but not expensive; masculine, but professional. She tore off the pant suit and attacked her closet.

Why the heck am I fussing?

Maggie barely knew the man, though she felt comfortable in his presence, even talking about the most painful part of her life. Maybe that was it: it was a relief to have someone willing to talk about what was on her mind every day of her life. Too many people avoided the topic of Jenna at all costs.

Maggie saw in her head the detective's soft brown hair, trim and wiry body, and large cow eyes that were somehow both attractive and soothing. If only she'd experienced a small part of that kind of comfort when she was with Chad. Then, even if the marriage was doomed, the two of them could have helped each other get through all this. Chad had never been one to "talk things over," and after Jenna went missing, he became defensive, combative, and even more closed off.

Maggie sat down on her bed in panties and bra. Then she did something she rarely did these days: she gave in to the grief that hung over her head. She lay back against the pillows and covered her face with her hands.

For a full ten minutes she lay silently, her shoulders shaking, her hands getting wet. She wasn't even thinking about why she was crying, but the action exhausted her. Her hands came down to her sides. Her eyes closed.

Maybe I should cancel dinner. I'm just too tired.

By the time Maggie woke, it was 6:30 p.m. – much too late to cancel the meeting with Sam, even if it was just an informal dinner.

She rose, splashed water on her face, went to the closet, took out an old lavender dress she'd always loved for its soft flowing comfort, and dressed, feeling a bit better and ready to face the next step: searching for her daughter with help from a hired professional.

In another neighborhood of Lancaster, Sam Osborne's mind was also whirring about the case and about dinner. Strangely, he found the specifics of the case kept giving way to images of his client. He'd asked her to dinner mostly to discuss this case, but he had to admit he was looking forward to spending an evening getting to know Jenna's mother. He had never seen color quite the shade of either her hair—it reminded him of the beach line just as water hit sand—or the eyes—a shade so intense it was hard not to want to get lost in them. Because of her athletic build, she fit into her clothes like a hand fit into the right-sized glove. While some might call her too thin, Sam had always admired woman that were trim, but gently muscled.

Sam admitted to himself then, that though she was not a classic beauty, she was definitely a looker, in his eyes anyway. He also knew, however, that his desire to spend time with her went beyond the pleasure of her physical appeal. Their few brief conversations revealed a level of fierceness that intrigued the detective. He was looking forward to learning more.

If this were not a dinner to discuss a case, Sam would have wished it were a date. He shook his head at the thought. Sam had done his fair share of seeing women since his divorce many years ago. He'd been on only a few formal dates though. He was just much more comfortable with women who could get beyond the initial awkwardness and enjoyed just hanging out and doing everyday things together. Sam had remained friends with a few of the women he'd dated, those who could get beyond the desire to marry. He had no desire to tie the knot again, but he did like female company.

Sam shook his head as he opened his closet door.

Why am I even thinking about this now?

He was taking Maggie to his favorite Chinese restaurant, and while it didn't require fancy attire, he had always felt as comfortable in tie and coat as his trusty jeans. He tried and failed to focus his thoughts on selecting clothing for the evening. His son, Davie, and the parallels of the two kidnappings were stronger pulls—stronger even than thoughts of his attractive new client.

Sam sighed deeply, his hand halfway into the closet.

I never should have taken this job.

Like with Chad and Maggie, the disappearance of his son had torn a rift in his marriage, which had ended in bitter divorce. Sam took a large share of the blame on himself, knowing he'd spent too much of his life after the kidnapping on trying to find a son who was probably dead. It was why he understood the root of Maggie's determination.

Sam grabbed a blue tie and an old comfortable chocolate-colored sport coat and went to stand in front of his mirror.

It was just a client meeting. He was a professional. He would ask the right questions, poke into the right corners and hopefully at least get a few answers for Maggie.

He was at Maggie's door exactly at seven.

Sam and Maggie arrived at Mrs. Wong's Eatery fifteen minutes later. He knew almost immediately that he'd chosen well. The bustle of the wait staff as they served the crowded restaurant was at just the right level to create a feel of hominess, and he could see Maggie relax. The staff laughed and talked with each other as well as with customers, as they weaved in and out of the widely spaced tables. Yet the noise level of restaurant didn't overwhelm conversations at individual tables. It was a good place to enjoy both scrumptious food and talk.

Sam grinned when Maggie tried to use chopsticks to pick up rice, but gave her credit for trying. Maggie laughed when Sam took a first bite of orange chicken and mistakenly got a pepper. He grabbed for his water glass, his eyes spilling tears at the spiciness. For the first hour of the evening, the two didn't talk about the case. They skimmed along on the surface of conversation, getting to know each other, occasionally dipping a toe a little deeper into a topic. Sam asked Maggie about her job as a real estate agent and what the market was like. Maggie explained why she loved the act of closing on a house: a new beginning for a family, a clean slate for an individual with a new job.

Maggie was fascinated by Sam's police background and pumped him for information on what it was like to deal with true criminals on a daily basis.

Without acknowledging it verbally, the two seemed to agree they needed time away from the tragedy that brought them together. But the case eventually caught up to them. While sipping a final cup of tea, Sam got down to business.

"Tell me about some of your neighbors, Maggie. How well do you know them?"

"You mean like Dottie Alstead and the Stewarts?" she asked, knowing he'd been to visit them that day.

"Any of the people from the neighborhood. I know police questioned everyone, but the investigation focused heavily on the mall where she was taken."

Maggie sat back in her chair and set her teacup on the table.

"Oh, Sam. I know everyone is a suspect, but I can't see any of my neighbors involved in something like this!"

"Tell me anyway."

"Well, as you no doubt discovered, I went to school with Dottie. It's a just a coincidence we ended up on the same street."

Maggie studied her tea.

"Dottie was a busy body even in school. She always seemed to know what was going on. She's a pretty good neighbor though, I guess. Greeted us when we first got there. Kept up with what was going on with Jenna. But after her husband died, she just seemed to spend most of her time gossiping about neighbors. I know she means well…" Maggie was quiet.

"But she's one of those people who feed off the sensationalism," Sam finished for her.

Maggie looked up from her teacup, surprised. A smile played on her lips.

"Yes, I guess that's exactly it. She's always on my doorstep mere seconds after the police or the media or practically anyone she doesn't know comes knocking at my door. I swear she has a sixth sense."

"And the Stewarts across the street?" Sam prodded.

"Oh, they're one of those couples who seem to be a fixture in the neighborhood. Like Dottie and her husband, they were living there when Chad and I moved in. Mrs. Stewart brought me a coffee cake on the day we moved."

"No children?" Sam asked. He poured himself another sip of tea.

"No, not of their own. I think, though, that they had a niece or grandniece or someone that frequently visited. I saw the girl a couple of times when Chad and I first moved there, then didn't see her again. I remember seeing little girl toys in the house."

"And did you ever meet the neighbor that rented the house next to the Stewarts—Albert was his name, according to Mrs. Stewart."

Maggie was silent for a few moments. She studied her teacup again, as if weighing what to say.

"We weren't formally introduced, no. And he wasn't there long. He also wasn't around much. I waved a few times, but I think he liked to keep to himself."

She was quiet again. Sam didn't prod. He just waited out the silence. Maggie ran one hand through her hair, and then looked into Sam's eyes.

"I didn't share this with police early on, Sam, because I didn't really think about it at all. I mentioned it several days after the investigation to an FBI agent following up on neighbors, then felt foolish."

Sam remained silent.

"This is probably not fair to the poor fellow, and it's based on instinct and one incident, but he gave me the creeps."

"What incident was that, Maggie?"

"It was a gorgeous spring day, and Jenna

and I were playing catch in the yard. I got tired and sat down on the porch, but Jenna kept tossing the ball, then chasing it down. Once, she let it go a little too close to the street and I jumped up and ran after her calling her name. I happened to glance up as I was bringing Jenna and the ball closer to the house, and I saw him."

"Saw him?"

"He must have been staring out the window at Jenna. He looked startled when I spotted him, then let the curtain drop without waving. I'm certain now it meant nothing."

Maggie's furrowed brow showed Sam she didn't really think it was nothing.

"Did authorities look into him?"

"I'm pretty sure the local police interviewed him at the time of the incident. The FBI agent who I talked to looked at me as if I was reaching for straws, which I probably was."

Maggie tilted her head as if she was absorbing her last statement and forcing herself to believe it.

"It doesn't hurt to look into it further, Maggie," Sam said, startling his dinner companion. She smiled broadly.

"Thanks."

Sam took a sip of tea and set it down gently.

"Is there anyone else on your street that you

know well or that had contact with you, Chad or Jenna?"

Maggie looked rueful.

"To tell you the truth, I didn't get to know my neighbors very well. The Stewarts live right across the street. Dottie I knew from high school. There were several families who had small children that Jenna had play dates with. I'll give you a list, but I don't know them well and haven't spoken to them since the kidnapping."

"You and Chad weren't the socialites of the neighborhood?" Sam asked. Maggie laughed, erasing any sign of regret on her face.

"Hardly. We did the barbecue bit a couple of times early in the years we were first there. I think Chad agreed only to see if he could drum up some insurance business. He had his own group of buddies from work that he hung out with and sometimes played poker with. I have a few friends I've made over the years, but they aren't neighbors, and I'm not really the type to go out much. Jenna kept me pretty busy."

Suddenly, her face clouded.

"It's terrible, Sam."

He raised his eyebrows in inquiry.

"The child in Allentown. What those parents are going through. I feel like I should call the parents, and tell them I know what an empty place is growing inside of them. I realize that's foolish and would do no good. But I feel their pain right now. Have the police found anything?" A tear had formed in her eye. She quickly dashed it away.

Sam shook his head.

"No, Maggie. Not that my sources have told me. It's a similar case to Jenna's in that the child, a little boy, was snatched from a mall store. I don't have much else, however. I promise I'll look into any connections I find and tell you what I can."

He reached over and covered her hand.

"You're right, though. You couldn't really say anything to them at this point that would help."

After dinner, Sam and Maggie walked. They had no destination in mind, but the neighborhood had a pocket park, the sky had a million stars, the evening breeze was cool and gentle. It was the perfect dessert to a full and satisfying meal. For much of the walk they said nothing, the silence comfortable and soothing after hours of conversation.

At ten, however, Maggie brought up work the next day and Sam drove her home. Sam insisted on walking Maggie to the front door where they felt the first moment of awkwardness during the evening. When Maggie inserted the key and turned back to Sam, the reality hit both at about the same time.

Although we can't call it one, this felt like a date.

Maggie's honesty bubbled to the surface, though she didn't use the d-word. "Thank you for the evening, Sam. I haven't enjoyed myself or been so relaxed in a very long time," she said quietly. "I really needed this."

"I did, too. I just didn't realize it." He was staring at her lips, but he knew better than to act. It may have felt like a date, but Maggie was his client.

CHAPTER ELEVEN

SAM SLEPT THROUGH THE night, free of thoughts of kidnappings and kids. He woke up smiling and leaped out of bed to confront his reflection in the mirror. He waggled his finger at his face.

"You're not fooling yourself, Sam Osborne. You know you can't do a thing about it, but you like her, and I think she knows it." He tried to shake off the foolishness, and then realized there was no need.

When Sam greeted Casey, the smile was still plastered to his face.

"My, but we're chipper this morning," she commented. Sam immediately sobered.

"I have to look over my notes and make a

few calls," he said in an even tone. "Then I have lots of research for you."

He went to the coffee machine, poured a giant mug full of strong brew, went into his office and picked up the phone, perching just at the edge of his desk.

Sam called police headquarters and asked to speak to Captain McCoy.

"Good morning, Bob. Look at your calendar and let's pick a day for that burger."

The two got together at least once a month to swap stories on what was happening in their lives, as well as what the police department was focusing upon and what Sam had heard or seen on whatever case he was looking into. The talks had yielded leads and ideas for where to take an investigation for both men.

"I wanted to ask you something about the Turner case, Bob. What did the police find out about Culver, the man who lived in the home where the Stewarts reported a car in the street?"

"We interviewed the guy, Albert Culver, right after we talked to the Stewarts, and we called his employer to verify that he was at work the day of the kidnapping," Bob said. "Many people saw him throughout that day, so we know he was where he said he was." Then he chuckled. "The man was parking his car in the street to keep the driveway clean."

"Pretty thoughtful of a renter to avoid getting oil on the driveway," Sam commented.

Bob cleared his throat.

"I guess he was just fastidious. We verified that he was renting the place, there for a temp job to run the second shift of a construction crew and was gone just after the kidnapping. Several neighbors mentioned the guy was withdrawn and not friendly, but we had no reason to pursue it other than gossip."

Sam was nodding his head as Bob spoke. "I don't think he really had anything to do with the kidnapping, but I'll have Casey do a little deeper digging on all the neighbors," Sam said.

He knew Bob liked to hear those words. Although the Lancaster police department had followed procedures, manpower didn't always allow them to focus as sharply on specifics or dig as deep as Sam could do, and the FBI shared only what they thought local police needed to know. Sam had often stepped in at the local level to provide additional research power.

Sam then asked Bob if the department had any information on the Allentown case.

"I know it's probably far-fetched, but I'd like to see what authorities in that case can release to me, so I can see if there are any parallels," he said.

Bob laughed. "I can tell you one similarity, Sam, but it isn't to your advantage. The same FBI field agent in charge of Jenna's case is working with the Allentown police force on this Allentown thing. The guy was certainly competent from what I could tell. But he wasn't exactly a wealth of information to my department, so good luck getting in touch with him. You might have better luck with the police department there. You know a couple of the guys on the force, don't you?"

Sam then called detective Pete Bicker of the Allentown police force. While Sam didn't get much new information out of Bicker, largely because the detective's time was scarce, he received just enough to wonder about the similarities with Jenna's case.

Like Jenna, the boy had been taken from a clothing store where he'd been shopping, in this case with his father. The boy had been a few years older, but the circumstances had been the same. His father had been distracted by something at the cash register. He'd turned back to the boy and discovered him missing, then frantically searched the store and the mall without finding anything.

The demand for a ransom had been almost immediate, though no bag was left at the front door of the home. In this case, the ransom had been put together by the parents before FBI or authorities were even alerted—the demand had been made by direct cell phone call to the parents. The amount was fairly small: $500,000. The parents had somehow convinced mall security to keep still for a few hours to make the drop-off themselves, and then alerted the police when the boy was not returned.

But the similarities stopped there. The couple that had lost their son had been wealthy, so the money had been easy to come by. The strangest part of all, however, was that there was no pickup for the ransom. The kidnappers had never fulfilled their promise to collect, just as they'd never fulfilled the promise to return the boy. Instead, they'd simply maintained silence while the parents came forward and began appeals on television.

Sam had seen those appeals. While he had trained himself to be suspicious of everyone, he couldn't help feeling sorry for the parents as their hollow eyes pleaded with the kidnappers to give them some word, *any* word about their son.

The next call Sam made was to Gretchen Myers Real Estate, the company that rented out the Anderson house to Albert Culver. A cheerful voice answered the phone, and Sam was surprised to find out Ms. Myers answered her own phone. Sam explained what he was working on and asked for details on Culver.

"As I told the police, the guy paid for two months on that house upfront, almost $3,000. But he left me in the lurch for the last three months he said he'd be there. I didn't make him sign a lease because he paid in cash, and Mrs. Anderson okayed it. She was visiting family in Europe and just wanted someone in the house. Culver wasn't sure how long his temp job would last, but my notes say he intended to stay until June or July."

"How long after the Turner kidnapping did he leave?" Sam asked. "The kidnapping was March 7, 2009."

"Just a minute," she told Sam. "I'll check the records."

Almost 10 minutes went by with Sam on hold, and he was just wondering whether to hang up and call back when Gretchen Myer's voice came on the line.

"Sorry about that, Mr. Osborne. Got a call on my cell while I was on my computer. Let's see... I'm not exactly sure when his boxes disappeared. He rented the house on January first. I tried calling him beginning about March tenth about March's rent, and then went by to try to collect rent on March thirtieth, but that's as far as our records go. I had someone from my office go by the first week in April, and that employee reported that the man was completely gone, the front door left unlocked. Mrs. Anderson chose to take no further action because there was no lease and she was returning that fall."

"The police or FBI didn't ask you for a forwarding or a former address?" Sam asked.

"Yes, I believe they did. I had no forwarding address as I recall, and I didn't need to check the former address personally, Mr. Osborne. He gave me the name of the company he was consulting for as a reference, and I checked up on that by phone before renting to him. I have dealt with that firm many times because they fly people in as specialists. The job he was working on must have ended earlier than he thought, and I guess he decided to stiff us for those last few promised months."

Sam thanked the woman and hung up. He sat down at his office, scribbled a few notes, and then walked out of his office to Casey's desk. Her eyes lit up when she saw his office notebook. He had a habit of writing down his thoughts then having her pursue what he was thinking, and that was the fun part of her job.

"I want you to find out all you can about Selma and Daryl Stewart at this address," Sam said, ripping off a sheet. "I'm especially interested in whether or not they ever had a child or maybe took care of a niece."

Casey didn't ask why. She just took the slip of paper.

"And can you also please look into an embezzling case a few years back—at First Third Bank. I want to learn about the accused man's family."

"Sure, Boss. Sounds like a fun day," Casey chirped.

"Oh, you're not done yet. Take this name…" Sam handed her another scribbled scrap of paper with Albert Culver's information, "and see if, somewhere in this great nation of ours, you can locate him."

Casey's eyes lit up. She loved a good challenge.

"Also, see what you can find out about the people close to the kidnapping case from the Lehigh Valley Mall near Allentown. The store was Abercrombie and Fitch. The police won't release who was working that day, but see what you can do and check out some of the surrounding stores."

Casey gave Sam a wry smile.

"If it involves a mall and shopping, I'm on the case," she said. "I think my friend Sarah's sister lives near there. Maybe I can convince her to do a little reconnaissance shopping."

Sam chuckled and continued.

"Ask your hubby if he knows anyone else on the Allentown police force who might be willing to share a few more facts of the case. I've talked to the detective in charge, but got very little. Then check up on the parents of Benjamin Smithfield, the boy who went missing. Here are the names and the address." Sam reached over and handed her a third piece of paper. "I know the parents are fairly wealthy, but do a little poking around there, anyway. See if anything smells funny."

"Of course, Sam. But I've watched the television reports. I was almost in tears seeing them beat themselves up over not contacting police sooner. It is kind of bizarre, I know, that the money wasn't picked up."

"I agree," Sam said. "And it's not likely there's a connection, but we need to know as much as we can find out as outsiders."

Sam grabbed his jacket on the way out the door, but turned back to smile at his aid.

"Enjoy yourself, Casey. Cause I'm off to interview someone I am trying hard not to dislike."

CHAPTER TWELVE

SAM'S MIND CHURNED AS he drove to Chad's office for a formal interview. It wasn't often he was uncomfortable with someone, but he was having a hard time keeping an open mind about Chad Turner. Yes, Maggie's ex-husband had come storming angrily into Sam's office, but Sam had certainly dealt with his share of temper and testosterone.

Sam was pretty sure his real problem with Chad Turner was that he was Maggie's former husband and the father of a kidnapped child. Although Sam didn't know Maggie well, his mind could not envision the two of them as a couple. It made him uncomfortable and itching to know more about how they managed to stay together for the almost five years they were married.

He shook his head and rolled his eyes.

How in the heck could I judge them when I was together with the wrong woman for a decade?

The father issue was even more of a struggle. Sam knew the gut-wrenching, all-consuming guilt that accompanied being the father of a child who has disappeared. A father is supposed to protect; to keep his family safe. Chad had failed, just as Sam had failed, though he seemed to have moved on much more quickly than Sam had.

Sam didn't want to feel sorry for Chad or even try to understand why the man was so angry.

At least until I know for sure he isn't behind this crime.

Sam arrived at Chad's office promptly at 1 p.m. and waited in the lobby for ten minutes.

When Chad strode in, cool and crisp in business-blue pants, white shirt and blue tie, Sam was momentarily taken aback. The last time Sam had seen him, he appeared to have steam coming out of his pores. His face had been splotchy and red; his hair mussed.

Now Sam saw the Chad Turner everyone else saw. Black curly hair and sparkling baby-blue eyes topped a body that would make most men envious. Sam guessed Chad must carry about 230 pounds on his six-foot-two-inch frame, and he could see from the forearms peeking out of rolled up shirtsleeves that Chad probably spent a few hours at the gym. The firm handshake was accompanied by a wide smile that revealed perfectly aligned white teeth.

He looks like a magazine model, Sam thought.

"Sam Osborne," Sam said routinely, realizing after he said it that Chad knew who he was. After all, the man had a temper tantrum in Casey's office.

As if he could sense Sam's thoughts, Chad's smile faltered. "Sorry about the sudden appearance in your office yesterday. I was upset about Maggie hiring you, but I guess I should have calmed down before I came to see you." He turned and gestured towards an office as he added, "I haven't changed my mind about hiring you, however. I still think it's a worthless idea."

Once Chad was seated behind a giant desk and Sam was seated as well, Chad sighed and continued.

"I don't mean to sound callous, Mr. Osborne. But I truly believe Maggie is wasting her money on you, just as she did on all the other experts. Almost everyone thinks Jenna is dead, and as horrible as that makes me feel, I firmly believe that the authorities have done what they could. We've received no word in the two and a half years since the ransom was paid. Maggie needs to get on with her life and not waste what little money she has saved on hiring a detective."

Sam opened his notebook and looked up at Chad.

"Is there a particular reason you feel it's futile to search any further?"

A cloud passed over Chad's face.

"Are you insinuating something?"

Sam looked back down at his notebook.

"No. I'm just asking questions. It's what I do. I know you've been over all this, but let's begin with where you were the day she disappeared."

Chad rose slowly from his chair, startling Sam, who looked up again. Chad was breathing heavily, and Sam caught a second glimpse of the kind of temper the man had. The detective knew he'd learn very little from an angry interviewee.

He kept his tone even as he explained, "I'm only trying to piece the day's events together, Mr. Turner. I am not accusing anyone, nor do I even have an opinion yet what could have happened. I am just trying to put together a timeline of the kidnapping."

Chad sat, and Sam watched as he corralled his anger. The model's smile returned.

"Of course. I want to help in any way I can. I was with a client."

"Yes, that's what you told the police," Sam said nodding his head.

The temper was back, but at a lower simmer point. "And yet you felt you had to ask me again," Chad said through clenched teeth. "What are you hoping to learn here, Mr. Osborne?"

Sam put his pen down on his notebook and sat back in his chair.

"My job is to go beyond what the police had time for, Mr. Turner. If you could just go over the details again, you may think of something new."

"Oh, for Christ's sake," Chad said, running one hand through his hair. "This is utterly ridiculous. We've spent far too much time answering the same questions over and over. I was with an important client. He'll attest to my presence, again, if necessary."

He sat back in his chaired and glared.

"You know, of course, that the police were ready to brand me as the kidnapper."

"It's pretty standard to suspect family first," Sam said quietly.

Chad turned to his computer and fiddled with the keyboard trying to bring something up on his desktop computer. When he'd found what he was seeking, his finger rested on a spot on the screen.

"I was with Bob Applegate," he muttered. "1224 Cherry Lane. Area code five-five-five, six-seven-two, four-eight-six-six."

Sam knew that Applegate had affirmed Chad's whereabouts, but he wrote down the number anyway.

"Maggie says that you have a few friends you play poker with. Would it be possible to get their names, as well?"

"*What?* Now you want to check out my buddies? What the hell could they possibly have to do with someone snatching my kid?"

Sam looked up from his scribbling.

"I'm just looking around at possibilities, Mr. Turner. Maybe your friends have nothing to do with it, but they have information about you and maybe your family that could have been inadvertently passed along."

Chad drummed his fingers on his desk. "Okay. Whatever. I'll get you a list, but I want time to call them first and let them know who the hell you are."

"Fair enough," Sam said. Then he flipped through his notebook.

"I understand that you and your wife weren't getting along, even before the kidnapping."

Chad glared at Sam again.

"And just who the hell told you *that*? Has someone in that damn neighborhood we lived in been gossiping about our personal business? How I got along with my wife is none of their concern, or yours either, for that matter. You know we divorced. I don't really see how our rocky marriage relates to the kidnapping."

"If how you got along with your wife has nothing to do with what happened, you should be comfortable answering the question," Sam said calmly.

Chad Turner picked up a paperweight, then put it down. He fidgeted in his seat and appeared to be trying to get comfortable. Sam knew he was really giving himself time to weigh his answer. Sam saw the moment when Chad decided he might as well say what was on his mind.

Chad cleared his throat and sat back in his chair.

"Maggie and I didn't get along almost from the beginning of our marriage. She probably told you we dated when we were in high school. We didn't see each other for many years, and then met up later in life when she moved back to town from the city. I thought I was going out with the old Maggie when I asked her out. I didn't find out until later how manipulative living in a city had made her."

"We dated for a couple months, then she trapped me into marrying her," Chad said.

Sam looked up, surprise on his face.

"Trapped you?" he asked.

"Well maybe that's a poor choice of words. But we hadn't been together very long when she told me she was pregnant. I had to marry her."

Sam cocked his head. "Why?"

Chad narrowed his eyes at the question.

"I may not have been in love with her, but I cared for her, Mr. Osborne. She was my high school sweetheart. I felt I had to do the right thing."

He was playing with the paperweight again, studying it as if seeing it for the first time.

"In hindsight, I probably should have insisted on a paternity test. For all I knew, Maggie could have been sleeping around in Philly."

Oh, I doubt that, Sam thought to himself, trying to stem his own anger. He just couldn't see Maggie trapping a guy into marrying her or having multiple partners. Nor could he see her as someone who would agree to marry a guy who asked her to have a paternity test. But then, she'd married the guy for some reason, rather than facing being a single mom.

"And how did you feel about having a daughter?" Sam asked.

His question caused an entire change in Chad's demeanor. His face took on a faraway look, as if he were returning to his past. His posture relaxed for the first time since Sam had arrived.

"Once she was born, I didn't care if she was mine. She looked like me, laughed like me. So I pretty much accepted that she'd inherited her chiseled good looks from me." He was smiling broadly, and then he grew serious and looked into Sam's eyes. "I loved her, of course. She was a wonderful kid, and a daddy's girl. She was smart as a whip and coordinated as could be. I'm sure she would have excelled in sports. She also seemed mature beyond her years. Never put up a fuss when daddy couldn't play with her or had to be at the office instead of at home. I think she understood better than Maggie how much responsibility I was carrying with this job."

He was quiet for a few moments.

"I know that doesn't make much sense. But you'd have to have met her to understand."

He sat back in his chair and sighed.

"I miss her every day."

Chad sought out Sam's eyes as he added, "I may not have loved her mother, but I loved my Jenna-boo."

Sam held Chad's gaze, trying to gage whether the other man was lying. *He deserves an Oscar if he is*, Sam thought. He changed tracks in his questioning.

"Do you have any theories about who might have taken your daughter, Mr. Turner?"

Chad sat up straighter in his chair and straightened his tie.

"I do not for a second believe it was someone we know. The crime was well planned, according to police. But it could have been carried off by anyone who did the research." He cleared his throat before adding, "And despite the fact the police focused way too much time during those first few days trying to pin it on me, I had no reason to harm my own child for $250,000 of my own money."

Sam remembered what Maggie said about the fact the amount was initially scraped together by Maggie's father. Antagonizing Chad further by bringing that fact up served no purpose, however. After ten more minutes of questions, Sam rose. He would dig into Chad's past, but he didn't really think the man was guilty of much except being an ass.

"Thank you, Mr. Turner. I know this has been difficult for you and Maggie, and I know you don't agree with Maggie that I can help. But I want you to know that I intend to find Jenna if she is still alive—or some information on what really happened to her. I am not doing this for the money."

Chad's eyebrows rose. He didn't ask for

further explanation or thank Sam for his efforts. But he rose to his feet and reached for Sam's hand before walking the detective out.

CHAPTER THIRTEEN

"I'M AFRAID YOUR FORMER husband wasn't too happy to see me. I may have upset him." Sam didn't feel the need to mention to Maggie that her former husband also had stormed into Sam's office the day before Sam conducted his formal interview.

He looked around the restaurant, and then pulled out a chair for Maggie. She had selected their dining place this time: a cozy, comfortable family-run Italian cafe.

She smiled up at Sam as she sat. She wasn't used to such gentlemanly manners. It somehow went with the dress she'd picked out, a long flowery thing that was casual and old-fashioned at the same time.

"It doesn't take that much too upset Chad, I'm afraid. He's a passionate man who gets angry pretty easily," Maggie said.

Sam sat across from her and smiled crookedly. "Yes, I noticed the trigger temper. Does your husband treat all males like competition?"

"*Ex*-husband," Maggie corrected, as she picked up the napkin and placed it in her lap. "And the male macho bit is part of who he is, which is…well, you saw it," she said.

Sam picked up his own napkin, and then cleared his throat before asking the next question.

"He didn't get physical with you or Jenna, did he, Maggie?"

Maggie shook her head. "No, Sam. He did his share of storming out of the house, but he never touched either one of us."

Sam decided to be direct. "Do you think Chad could have had anything to do with this?"

Maggie folded her hands and rested them on the napkin in her lap before replying.

"Chad may not have been the one to care for Jenna when she was sick. He didn't take her to preschool or teach her the alphabet. He couldn't often be coaxed into playing a game with her. And if he did, it didn't last long. He had very little patience, and he was gone a lot. But he wasn't a bad father." She raised her head to gaze into Sam's eyes. "So no. I do not believe he had anything to do with this."

"Just had to ask, Maggie," Sam said softly. "He seems to deeply disapprove of all you've done trying to find your daughter, and I guess he feels I'm just the latest thing."

Maggie bowed her head.

"Well, I did go a little crazy, especially that first year. I'm afraid I spent a bunch of money on people who promised they could find her."

The two sat in comfortable silence, lost in their own thoughts for a few moments, until a waiter brought and poured a delicious, light white wine Maggie had ordered.

"And did you ever find out anything from those people you paid?" Sam asked over the lip of his wineglass.

Maggie's eyebrows lifted.

"I'm surprised you'd even ask. They were mostly quacks, and I think I saw them as much to feel like I was doing something as out of any real belief they would help. And sometimes, it just felt good to talk to someone who appeared for a few minutes to care. I didn't often go back to anyone, but I could write a book about how many people are out there that say they can make a connection with a missing loved one," she said somberly.

Then Maggie was quiet for a few moments, and Sam let the quiet settle in before prodding.

"Do you still consult with anyone?"

She raised her eyes from the table to Sam. Then she leaned forward slightly and covered Sam's hand with her own.

"I know that this sounds completely crazy, and I wouldn't blame you if you labeled me a nut, but yes. I returned several times to a woman who lives not far from Lancaster. I don't talk to her often—the last time was several months ago. I don't know what it is about her, but I always feel like she knows me somehow. She claims to be able to feel Jenna—to know she is alive. I know I shouldn't believe it…but I do."

Sam squeezed Maggie's hand before releasing it.

"I'm not here to judge. And none of us really understands what the human mind could do if we were more open to psychic waves or whatever it is these people think is out there. I think we should talk to the woman together if you're up for that."

Maggie smiled broadly. "Okay, Sam. If nothing else, it will be an interesting experience for you, I'm sure. Now, what else have you been up to?"

"I conducted a few interviews with people who live close to you or are affiliated with those close to you or Chad," Sam said.

"What did you think of my nosey friend, Dottie?"

Sam chuckled. "She is certainly forthcoming with her information. You know, I also talked to the Stewarts, to a few of the people on that list you gave me, and I've called and checked on some of Chad's poker buddies. I can't see a connection with anyone yet, but I'm checking on everyone's background, including your neighbors."

"The list of people I know is pretty pitiful these days," Maggie said. "I'm sure it will take you longer with Chad's list of friends. I'm afraid my ability to make friends and to have interesting things to say has grown a little rusty. "

"I think you are very easy to talk to," Sam said. He reached over and reclaimed Maggie's hand, startling her.

"Look, I know this isn't exactly professional. And it's really not like me to be forward. I want you to know, however, that I don't think I've ever had an easier time talking to someone. I certainly didn't have many heart-to-hearts with Barbara, my ex." He dropped her hand, sat back, and took another sip of wine.

"Tell me about her," Maggie said softly.

"The relationship, the marriage, the divorce was a long time ago. We were way too young when we met. We fell into a relationship based largely on hormones and a good time. We married not knowing each other. She continued to have a good time partying; I was a homebody. In the end, it did not work at all."

Sam gazed deeply into his wine glass.

"We had Davie and for a short time; we were a family. Not a very solid one, but we had the common love of being his parents."

"Davie?" Maggie asked. She'd seen the flash of pain in his eyes.

Sam silently cursed his slip. He hadn't intended to tell her about Davie. He didn't want her to see how stupid he was for taking this case, how personally he felt about the kidnapping of a child.

Still, he had no wish to lie.

"Davie was our son. He would be twenty this Christmas. He was kidnapped fourteen years ago, and it was my fault."

"Oh, my God!" she exclaimed. "Why didn't you tell me?"

"I probably should have. I wasn't ready to."

The waiter brought their food, but neither felt like eating. After a few bites, Sam pushed his plate back and said softly, "Let's walk."

They rose in unison, leaving mostly untouched food. Sam paid the bill and asked the waiter to box the leftovers. The two left and began to walk, letting the lovely, fall day wash over them like a cool breeze. The colorful leaves swirled at their feet. The air was chilly in that wonderful refreshing autumn way, not yet cold, but enough to create goose bumps. Maggie put her arm through Sam's. With bowed heads, they crossed the street and entered the park. They walked the entire length before Sam began to speak again.

"It was one week before Davie's sixth birthday. I promised I would take him shopping so he could spend the money he received from my great aunt," Sam began. "He picked out a badminton set at a giant sports shop he loved. We walked toward the cash register—me pulling out my wallet, Davie holding that box like it was some kind of treasure."

"At the register, the clerk said there was something wrong with my card. I handed over another, the clerk rang things up; I signed the slip and turned back to Davie."

Sam swallowed hard. His voice shook as he continued.

"He was gone, just simply gone. No one had seen where he'd gone—not the clerks, not the customers in line behind me. I began calling out his name. People in the store started searching. Someone called security, then the police. Everyone searched that area for hours, every store and restaurant, every possible hiding place. There were no signs of Davie, no witnesses, no leads. My boy was gone."

"Oh, Sam," Maggie cried softly. "You know."

"Yes," Sam agreed. "I certainly know what a terrifying, then soul-crushing thing it is you've been through and what a giant hole has been created in your heart."

They walked some more in silence. Sam finally stopped, let her arm drop and turned to face her.

"It's still horrible fourteen years later. I don't ever hear my doorbell without thinking 'It's Davie. Someone has come to bring me Davie.' Of course, it never is."

They resumed walking.

"Barbara divorced me a year later. All we had ever had in common was Davie so with him gone, we had nothing. She believes it was my fault; I believe it was my fault. A moment of distraction created years of misery and searching."

Again, Sam paused and turned to Maggie, the pain etched on his face. He wiped that face with one hand and sighed, dropping his chin to his chest.

"That's why I really didn't want to work on Jenna's disappearance and shouldn't have taken this job. Yet I couldn't say 'no,' but, please feel free to hire someone else. After all, I couldn't even find my own son."

Maggie reached over and took hold of Sam's

hand. With the other hand, she lifted his chin up, so she could look into his eyes.

"I want you on my side, Sam. You understand what I feel. You still have some hope in your heart." Then she leaned up and kissed his cheek, and the two continued their slow, steady walk.

CHAPTER FOURTEEN

NOSTALGIA SWEPT OVER HIM as he drove by the unplowed fields. Instead of piles of dirt, his mind saw rows and rows of corn stalks. The tall, straight plants had been the perfect place to hide and play when he and Eli were small. And the boys certainly deserved playtime since they spent many hours in back-breaking work planting, cultivating and harvesting that corn.

His life had been a hard one, though he hadn't realized how hard until he left it behind. Getting away from the labor and the constant grit under his fingernails had shown him that another way of life existed.

Had he ever believed in the simple lifestyle: the goodness of people, the possibility of a God watching over them? No, he could not remember truly believing. Nor had he believed that living the "clean life" would bring his parents the security or happiness they sought. He understood why they'd done it; in many ways, it was an easier way to live. Church members rarely stopped to try and figure out what happened to people when they died or to discuss the shades of gray that existed between "good" and "bad." They didn't have to address the issues because church doctrine gave them the answers.

The image of corn stalks from his past disappeared, and he saw the fields for what they were right then: muddy and empty. It wasn't yet time for planting.

The images in his mind switched from cornfields to Rebecca, his pretty, childhood friend with her shiny brown hair, huge eyes, and trusting ways. Like his parents, Rebecca had been gone from his life many years, lost to him because he'd simply been too young to confess his sins and marry her.

His mind shifted back to the present, and he glanced back at the sleeping child in the back seat of the car, a handsome lad with curly hair and striking features. Could the boy remember all he'd been taught in the last five days? Would the slender frame hold up to the labor that was surely to come?

He still couldn't figure out why he hadn't killed this child. Killing had never been a problem. His partner would be furious if she knew what he couldn't do. She'd probably take the money and run. He'd had to come up with an alternate plan.

The farms began to look familiar as he turned onto the road between Antwerp and Hicksville. After several miles, he turned off onto the hard-dirt-packed lane that had always brought the family home and parked a short distance from the buildings. Were his parents even still alive? Was Eli here?

Carrying the sleeping child in his arms, he walked to the barn. It was still dark outside—too early in the morning for the milking. He placed the child in the hay at the back of the barn. The boy stirred a little, but when he heard a whispered, "Go back to sleep," the youngster sighed softly and turned over.

The next hour crept by. Finally, the barn door creaked open, and a man dressed in black pants, white shirt and huge straw hat entered. The man began milking the three mooing cows. When he heard a whispered "Eli," he stood, upsetting his stool.

"Eli. It's Johann."

"Johann?" Eli repeated. "My brother,

Johann?" he looked around the barn in the dim kerosene lighting and spotted Johann sitting in a dark corner.

Johann stood from his perch on a bale. "Yes, Eli, it's me."

Eli recovered from his shock quickly, straightened his stool and sat, resuming his milking.

"I do not know what you are doing or what trouble you are in, but you know I cannot talk to you. You have been shunned."

"Just listen to me. I need your help. I know I have no right to ask anything of you, but there is no one else I trust. Will you at least listen?"

Eli nodded his head, saying nothing.

"I am truly sorry for what I did to Rebecca. I did love her, but I was a child."

Johann paused then, not sure what to say next. "Is she all right, Eli?"

Eli nodded his head and, despite the shunning, spoke, "I married her, Johann. What else could I do? You disgraced our name."

Silence filled the barn, as Eli let that statement sink in. He looked over toward Johann in the shadows as he continued.

"Rebecca had a hard time with the birth. She almost died, and the child did not live. She is now barren. God's punishment for her sins…"

Johann shook his head at the irony of why he had made this journey.

"I'm sorry. Truly I am. She deserved to have lots of children. You deserve to have lots of children."

"God didn't see it that way. And here I am, sinning again by talking to you." His head turned back to his milking.

"What is it you want of me? Please say what you must say and leave us in peace."

Johann sat down again on his bale of straw and breathed deeply to fortify himself.

"My wife died a few months ago," Johann said. "We have a son, who is a good boy. I cannot take care of him properly or give him what he needs. I want him to grow up as we did, living the plain, good life. I want you to help me take care of him."

"You dare to ask Rebecca and me to take your own child!" Eli was talking through clenched teeth, but he did not stop the milking.

"He is your nephew. I'll send you money…"

Johann knew it was a stupid thing to say the second it was out of his mouth.

Eli rose to his feet, upsetting the stool again.

"We have no need of your ill-gotten gains. We have no need of anything of yours, including a child. How dare you even ask!"

Johann waited for just a few moments before he continued.

"I dare because I remember life on this farm. It was good; it was clean. We had what we needed; I was just too young to know it."

He approached Eli, but slowly. He only wanted to get Eli to look into his eyes.

"I love the boy, but I cannot give him the good life."

Eli moved from one cow to the next, taking his stool with him. He placed the stool carefully at the cow's side and sat. The only sound for a few minutes came from the ting of milk hitting the sides of the pail.

Finally, Eli picked up a full pail, turned to Johann and said, "May I see the child?"

Johann went back to the recesses of the barn and woke the boy. The child was rubbing his eyes as he approached Eli.

"What are you called?" Eli asked.

"Benjy. Benjamin. But Benjy for short."

Eli looked from child to brother. "Benjamin, it is. Wait here. I need to talk this over with Rebecca," he said.

In less than half an hour, he was back in the barn.

"It appears you will be part of our family, Benjamin. Say good-bye to your poppa, boy, and follow me into the house. Rebecca will give you some breakfast."

Eli did not look at his brother as he spoke. He turned and preceded the boy out the door. He did not see the look of relief on Johann's face.

CHAPTER FIFTEEN

SAM DREADED VISITING THE place where Jenna had been snatched. He knew it would bring back too much pain of his own as he studied the place where Maggie's misery began.

He also knew it would remind him of that exact moment of panic—that moment when Maggie's mind switched from focusing on everyday details to the reality that her child was not there. He'd been through that first hour after the initial realization, when frantic searching ruled everyone's actions, then was gradually replaced by desperation and finally despair. He understood how the hours after the child goes missing are a blur of conversations, police questions and nausea.

The main difference between the two kidnappings was that Sam waited for a ransom call that never came. It had never been clear why Davie was gone. Sam shuddered as he drove.

It took only ten minutes to get to the mall. Sam parked the car in front of the main entrance and made his way into Fran's Clothing Store.

"May I help you?" an elderly, white-haired woman asked Sam.

"I need to speak to the store manager. Is she or he available?"

"I certainly am. But I'm not up to a sales call this morning. We're expecting a crowd today."

The polite brush-off was accompanied by a smile enhanced by teeth too white and straight to be real.

"I'm not here on a sales call, Miss…?"

"I'm Francine Devonshire, the owner of this establishment and its manager."

Sam shook her hand.

"Sam Osborne, ma'am. I'm a private detective hired by Margaret Turner to look into the kidnapping of her child."

Francine's face lost its smile.

"I see." She bowed her head for a moment. When she raised it back up, she suddenly looked all 70 of her years.

"It was terrible, just terrible. Do you think we could talk about this in my office in back? Customers won't start arriving for a while. Would you like some coffee?"

Sam declined the coffee and followed her into a small office in a back room storage area for the store. He sat where she indicated and drew out his notebook.

"Were you the one waiting on Mrs. Turner that day?"

"Oh, no," she replied. "I greeted Maggie when she came in. I've known her for a long time, but I was busy. I let Natalie Collins take over. It was my day to work back here in the office."

"Is Natalie here today?" Sam automatically glanced around him.

"She doesn't work here anymore. Hasn't for a long time."

"Do you know where she went to work, and how I could get in touch with her?"

Francine's forehead wrinkled.

"I'm afraid not. She left on vacation about three weeks after that traumatic day, and then never came back. I was never convinced that the whole incident didn't just upset her so much she couldn't stand to come back."

"Did you report to the police that she left work so soon?"

Francine looked thoughtful for a moment. "I had no reason to do that, Mr. Osborne. They interviewed her after it happened, of course. Like the rest of us, the kidnapping hit her really hard, and I encouraged her to take that vacation. She'd saved for it, and she'd talked about it for months. Said she and her husband were flying to someplace exotic and warm. I encouraged her to take it sooner, and I guess once she finally got there, she decided not to come back."

Francine paused before adding, "She never really was enthusiastic about her job, anyway, and I think Jenna's disappearance pushed her over the edge."

"Did you ever meet her husband?"

"Just once. He was very polite, very quiet, kind of handsome, if I remember right. He came into the shop once to pick her up for lunch."

Francine smiled at Sam then and straightened her posture, settling into the wooden chair.

"Do you know Natalie's background—where she was born, went to school, worked? She probably gave you all that information at the time you hired her."

"I didn't know that much about her, really. I'm afraid I don't do much socializing with my own employees. Trudy, my other clerk at the time, knew her better I think. But let me poke into the files…"

Francine went to her file cabinet and pulled out a file. She took out a sheet of paper, hesitated, and then handed it to Sam.

"I guess it's okay for you to see her application; the police took down some details."

When she handed him the paper, she chuckled and added, "I know I should be cleaning out these files. Both those girls have been gone a couple years. I'm afraid I'm a bit of a hoarder when it comes to paperwork. I am always afraid to throw something away."

Sam smiled back at her. "That can be handy when a detective comes calling. Okay if I borrow this app and maybe Trudy's for a bit?" Sam asked.

Francine nodded and got a second piece of paper from the file cabinet; Sam put the papers under his notebook and resumed his questioning.

"Did Natalie notice, or did you, perhaps, see anyone hovering around the child that day?" he asked.

"Mrs. Turner was the only customer here. It was a Wednesday, an off day for business at this mall, and Mrs. Turner and Jenna came in towards the end of the day."

"But you saw the child when they came in?"

"Oh, you couldn't miss that sweet one. She was lovely, and so full of laughter. She was having a great time playing hide and seek from her mother." Francine's smile returned, but disappeared again at Sam's next question.

"And you don't think she could have wandered out of the store while her mother was occupied?"

"I suppose. However, I knew the little girl well enough to know it wasn't like her to go running off. She played hide and seek, but she was never far away. Like I told police, if she got anywhere near the front door, I guess someone could have grabbed her. I can't believe she'd leave on her own or that she wouldn't have screamed."

"Did Natalie or any of your other employees ever mention having problems with Mrs. Turner or Jenna?"

Francine tilted her head slightly.

"No. I don't know why they would."

"But?" Sam prompted. He could sense Francine's hesitation.

"Well I always had the feeling that Natalie and Trudy didn't particularly care for Mrs. Turner. I heard them refer to her as uppity. But they had a tendency to poke fun at customers... when they thought I wasn't listening."

Francine used one finger to scratch the top of her head. "I know Maggie can be aloof. However, she came into the store a lot, and I gradually learned to like her. I guess Natalie and Trudy were too young to take the time, or they just didn't get that chance."

"Were you in your office the entire time Natalie was waiting on Mrs. Turner?" Sam asked.

"Not at first. I saw them come in and went over to say hello, then left for my office."

"Can you see the mall door to the shop or the back door to the outside from this office?"

"No, not directly. But I quite possibly would see someone walking by on his or her way in and out the back of the store. As I remember telling the police, I was doing books, and I usually have the office door almost all the way closed to shut off some noise. I didn't open it fully until I heard Mrs. Turner fretting."

Sam asked a few more questions, and then requested a look around the shop. He noted the dressing room at the rear of the public shop, a short distance from the entrance to the back room. That back room was a large space with the office boxed off by thin walls on the opposite wall from the entrance to the shop. An exit to the parking lot was at the back of the big room in the center. Francine followed Sam as he examined it all.

Pointing at the exit, he turned to Francine and asked, "Would an alarm go off if someone tried to get in that door?"

"Oh, yes. You can access it only by key from the outside, although it unlocks automatically when the fire alarm goes off. I keep the door alarm set during the day."

"You keep the door locked and an alarm set during the day, even when you're working?" he asked.

"Always. I feel better knowing no one can walk in or break in through the back. To open it from the inside, you have to put a code into the box. On the outside, however, you have to have a key to get in. Once you're inside, you have to reset the code so the alarm doesn't go off."

"How many keys for getting in are there? Do employees have them?"

"I have allowed only a handful of people over the years to have a key. I can't seem to keep people employed long enough to trust them. And then I have one, of course."

"So Natalie and Trudy did not have a key?"

"No. When someone has morning shift, I either arrange to let them in at a certain time or have the alarm off long enough for them to arrive, then set it for the day."

"So you don't think either of your employees at the time could have gained access to your key?"

"I'm a stickler about it, Mr. Osborne. There's too much employee turnover in this business to give each clerk a key. And I keep my key in a safe in my office and get it out each night before I leave. I'm almost always the last to leave."

"So your employees are never alone in the store?"

"I sometimes leave early, but I take that key with me. The employees know that once they walk out the back door they can't get back in."

"So what happens when you have a day off or are sick?"

"I pride myself on never being sick. And I'm in every day at least part of the day."

She tilted her head then. Sam just sat silently.

"But you know, I think I *did* lend Trudy the key for a short time, though I got it back in just a few days. I went to visit my sister, who broke her ankle and was having trouble adjusting to getting around. I didn't want to close up shop, so I let Trudy do the openings since she'd been here the longest. But it was just two mornings… I don't think I told the police any of this. Do you think Trudy had something to do with this?"

"I'm not sure. But does Trudy still work here, too?"

"Nope. I'm afraid not. She also left a couple weeks after the kidnapping. I think she got an opportunity at a bigger department store."

Francine wrote the name of the store on a slip of paper and handed it to Sam.

"Would you mind opening the door for me?" Sam asked.

Francine went to retrieve her key, and then Sam followed her to the exit. Francine coded a number into the alarm system, stepped outside, then used the key to open the door and return. She reentered a code before the alarm could go off.

Francine shook Sam's hand again at the store's mall entrance. Before he could leave, however, she had a last comment.

"Do you really think Natalie or Trudy had something to do with the kidnapping? They were immature, but I can't believe either would do something so evil as taking a child."

Sam didn't answer. He just smiled again and thanked her for her cooperation. He gave her his card, and then left—satisfied he knew just a bit more, including how Jenna could have been taken from the store.

CHAPTER SIXTEEN

SAM AND MAGGIE ARRANGED to meet Monday on the outskirts of Lancaster for lunch. Sam wanted to visit the psychic Maggie had mentioned and get a feel for whether she could have anything to do with the kidnapping. He already had Casey checking the woman's background. He wasn't really expecting to find anything given the fact that Lucinda Lovejoy had come into the picture after the snatching and by Maggie's choice. He was puzzled why Maggie would feel like the woman knew her.

Other than a small placard with a white palm print and the words, "Psychic Readings" on it, Lucinda's house looked remarkably every-day—a small cape cod with green shutters and lush landscaping.

Besides her extra-sensory capabilities, the woman or whoever lives with her must have a green thumb, Sam thought.

Lucinda greeted Maggie like an old friend, throwing her arms around her shoulders and pulling her into an embrace. The woman wasn't much older than Maggie or Sam. She wore an outfit that fit her role of psychic: a long, silky, multi-colored skirt and a white eyelet-lace blouse. Her gray hair was pulled back in a barrette. Sam wondered if the gypsy-look was for show or truly reflected her taste in clothing.

"It's been too long, my dear. I've missed our chats," Lucinda said, pulling back away from Maggie and then studying her face.

"You look better. Relaxed. Almost happy." Lucinda said, and then she turned to study Sam.

"Is this your new friend?" she asked Maggie. Maggie nodded, looking slightly embarrassed.

Sam wondered what she had said about him.

"You didn't ask whether Jenna was back," Sam said to Lucinda.

"I don't have to. She's well. She's healthy. But she's not at home," Lucinda said, a sharp edge to her tone. She turned and walked back into her house, gesturing over her shoulder for the two visitors to follow.

The inside of the home was warm and inviting, decorated in feminine colors with old-fashioned-looking flowered wallpaper. Lucinda led them into a living room where Sam and Maggie sat down side by side on an overstuffed couch.

"Tea, my dears?" Lucinda asked. The pot was already steeping on the maple coffee table. A plate of biscuit-style cookies sat beside the pot.

"Is that your wonderful blackberry tea?" Maggie asked.

Lucinda was already pouring a cup. She handed one to Maggie, then raised her eyebrows at Sam.

"Yes, that would be nice, thank you, Ms. Lovejoy."

"Oh, no need for the formalities. Please call me Lucinda."

"And you can call me Sam," he said.

After the three were settled, teacup saucers on their laps, Lucinda spoke again. "Now why have you come to visit me, detective?"

"I understand Maggie has been coming to see you for a while, and I just wanted to ask a few questions."

"And you think maybe I had something to do with the kidnapping," Lucinda said, no unpleasantness in her voice. It wasn't a question.

Maggie gasped.

"Of course not, Lucinda! We would never think that. I'm sure Sam is just here to…"

"I suspect everyone," Sam interrupted, meeting Lucinda's gaze. "That's my job."

"Yes. And you're very good at it," Lucinda said. She cocked her head. "And you believe, like Maggie does, that Jenna is alive."

Maggie glanced from Lucinda to Sam, a look of query on her face.

"I am working from that assumption, yes," Sam said. "But I haven't made any decisions on how I feel."

"Yes, you have, Sam. Even if you don't realize it. Now what is it you want to know?"

Sam took a sip of tea, and then reached for a biscuit. He dipped the biscuit in his tea and took a small bite.

"Maggie's right. This tea is very good. Thank you, Lucinda."

Lucinda simply smiled, waiting for more.

"What is it like to feel someone's presence, the way you feel Jenna?" Sam asked, surprising himself. He hadn't really planned to ask her anything except how she and Maggie had developed a friendship. "Is it like a dream where you see her in your mind? How do you know that she's okay?"

Lucinda tilted her head, then put her teacup and saucer on the coffee table and leaned back into her chair.

"I find it very hard to describe to someone

who has not had these feelings exactly how they come to me. It's not always something I can control, and it doesn't just happen with people who ask me to try. It isn't something I see. It's simply something I feel. It also only happens with certain people."

"So you didn't know when I came to you whether it would work or not?" Maggie asked.

"No, Maggie. If you'll remember, I took a small fee at that first meeting, but we didn't settle on a regular amount until after we'd talked for a while; you'd brought me something of Jenna's and I'd been to your house to visit her room."

"But you did charge her a regular fee?" Sam asked.

Lucinda turned from Maggie to Sam and frowned.

"This is how I make my living, Sam. If I believe I can alleviate someone's suffering somehow, I charge them for the service."

"I meant no disrespect," Sam said. "I am just trying to get a feel for how this all works."

"As Maggie has no doubt told you, she visited me for about a year, probably about once every couple weeks, coming to me when she wanted to feel close to Jenna."

"And in all that time, you've not felt anything that could help us actually find her?" Sam asked.

Lucinda bowed her head and closed her eyes.

"Several times when this feeling came to me that Jenna was alive, I have felt her reaching out. I know this sounds peculiar, but I know that her hands are rough. I don't understand what that means, and I can't see how it would help, but it was a definite feeling," Lucinda said.

"Have you felt physical contact with other people you're reaching out to?" Sam asked.

"No, I can't say I have. But then, I can't say that I've had this strong a connection with anyone I've been trying to contact mentally," Lucinda said.

"Why do you think that is?" Sam asked. He was starting to think this woman truly believed in what she was saying.

"I do not know. I just do not know," Lucinda said. She was shaking her head, a sad look on her face.

"I wish I could tell you more. I wish I could see her in my mind. I'm so close, but I don't see anything. I just feel her."

"And how do you know it's her?" Sam said.

"Because it's not really me she's reaching out for. It's Maggie. I only feel her presence when Maggie is in the room—when Maggie is sad and needs to feel Jenna."

CHAPTER SEVENTEEN

SAM SAT AT HIS desk trying to focus on the case. His mind, however, wanted to wander. This case stirred up feelings he hadn't had in a long time. He kept returning to the day when Davie was snatched—the awful feeling of helplessness Sam hoped to never experience again.

He kept seeing Davie as he'd been that year before he disappeared wearing one of the t-shirts designed to look like a baseball team uniform. Davie had loved all things related to sports. The store where he'd disappeared had been one of his favorite places.

Had whoever taken him given him to a father who shared that passion? Was he even alive?

Sam shook his head. It had been years since he'd been this obsessed with the questions he couldn't find answers to.

It had also been years since his mind had been focused on a woman the way Maggie kept popping into his head. It wasn't just that he sympathized with her plight. He couldn't figure out why her mental image was so etched on his brain—why he seemed to notice little things about her like the way she tossed her hair. For some women, a toss was a show of vanity or flirtatiousness. For Maggie, it was connected to concentration. Whenever they were deep in a conversation, discussing the case facts and the possibilities of what could have happened, she flicked her hair in impatience, as if it had no right to get in the way of her thoughts.

Then, there were the gentle curves of her trim body, and the way her breasts rose when she flicked her hair...*oh, this is ridiculous.*

Sam stood up, walked around his desk and sat down again. He got file cards and went to his white board. He wrote down the names of the people who had entered the picture. Any one of them could be a suspect at this point. Neighbors Selma and Daryl Stewart, Albert Culver and Dorothy Alstead; childhood rival Nancy Maddox; store clerks Natalie Collins and Trudy Wilson; store owner Francine

Devonshire; and of course, Chad Turner. Even Lucinda made the list until Casey's research proved she couldn't be connected.

Sam called his assistant into the office. She had requested a few minutes with Sam so she could give him a report on what she'd found out so far.

Casey wheeled into the office, notebook in hand.

"The Stewarts don't have a child living with them, Sam. I called all the neighbors to double check. The local schools have no child registered under their name. The Stewarts were not born here in Pennsylvania, nor did they have a child born here. They lived for a while in Maryland, but the county where they lived had no birth records for a child either. Do you want me to look further?" Casey asked.

"Try neighboring states for births. I distinctly heard them talking about 'keeping the child' away. It might be a relative, and it probably has nothing to do with Jenna's disappearance, but check it out, anyway."

Sam sat back in his chair and stroked his chin.

"Also, check out specialized and private schools. Maybe the child is not attending a public facility. What did you find out about the Maddox family?"

Casey flipped through some pages.

"I was just in the midst of reading what I could on the embezzlement. There's a little bit online from regional coverage, but as you know, the Lancaster Press itself hasn't gotten far in archiving papers. The library, however, has it all on microfiche. I got what I could and am taking notes as I go. Or would you prefer to read it all yourself?"

Sam smiled warmly. Casey's investigative skills, which included drawing up possibilities as she did her research, were coming along beautifully.

"Let's try both. Bring in the articles with your notes."

As Casey wheeled out to retrieve her file on the Maddox's, Sam picked up the phone and made an appointment.

Half an hour later, Sam was sitting across from Roger Baker, owner of Baker & Sons Construction.

"What kind of worker was Culver?" Sam began. He'd alerted Baker why he was investigating a former project staff member. Roger had pulled a file on the job and was looking through the paperwork.

"It's been a few years, so all I can tell you is what the site manager reports and paperwork say. Al was a roofing specialist hired to oversee an office building that had some challenges associated with incorporating solar panel cells to tap into that power source. As far as I can see, he was always on time, a good supervisor of those under his watch. We were pretty much working 24/7 on the project to get it done on a tight deadline, and the roofing people usually had second shift."

Bill flipped through some pages towards the end of the file.

"It says here that his portion of the job finished early and that he was given the choice of whether to stay or leave and go back to his hometown."

"So he didn't leave before the job got finished?" Sam asked.

Roger was still flipping through the job jacket.

"No, I don't believe he left before he was supposed to."

Roger sat back in his chair, put the file on his desk and rested one hand on his ample belly.

"Once a job gets to a certain point, Mr. Osborne, the manager of whatever portion of the project that's done has a choice whether to stay on and get paid a little extra to make sure nothing beyond that point messes up the work… or go on to other jobs. Most stay to get the extra pay, of course. But maybe he elected to leave for another job."

"Do you have a forwarding address for Mr. Culver?"

Roger leaned over to pick up the file again. He pulled out the page and copied down some information to hand to Sam.

"This is the company that referred Al to us and where he would have gone on to another project."

Sam looked at the paper. It read: JJ Roofing & Sons, Park City, Utah. Alfred Kulvert.

Either the neighbors and the realtor had the wrong name or Albert Culver has an alias, Sam thought.

Back in his office, Sam called the roofing company's headquarters only to find out Alfred Kulvert was a name in the human resources records, but he was no longer employed there and hadn't been since the job in Lancaster. He handed the paper with the name on it to Casey to track down, then returned to his desk and picked up the phone.

Trudy Wilson had been easy to find. She had gone on to work at another clothing store not far from the mall and still lived with her parents in the Lancaster area. Her employer verified that Trudy still worked there, hired away from Francine's about two months after the kidnapping. With her employer's permission, Sam made an appointment to take her away from the job later that day to ask a few questions.

Natalie Collins was not so easy. All she'd really left behind was the address where she lived when she'd worked at the store. She had rented in nearby York, Pennsylvania. Sam picked up the phone again to call her landlord.

"Yea, of course I remember that kid getting taken," Trudy Wilson said, as she sipped her double shot caramel-macchiato. "It was a big deal for a while. I even talked to a television reporter, though they shaved it down to just a couple sentences on the news."

Trudy was one of those twenty-somethings influenced, but not consumed, by Goth. Her hair, which was obviously dyed dark-red, black eyebrows, and dark lipstick contrasted sharply with pale skin. A tattoo of something that Sam guessed might be a dragon crept up the side of her neck. A gold nostril ring matched the gold bracelets on her wrists and in both ears.

"I thought the kid was dead. Why are you talking to me now?"

"Jenna Turner was never found. I'm just following up on some things for her mother."

Trudy's forehead wrinkled. "Yeah, poor thing. She was really a mess on the news. Made me feel kind of sorry for all the times Natalie and I poked fun of her behind her back. She may have been a snob, but… well. No one deserves having your kid grabbed."

"Natalie and you did not like Mrs. Turner?" Sam prodded.

Trudy took another sip, weighing her response.

"We didn't really know her, just didn't care for her type. Talking about customers was just something to do with Natalie. We made fun of a lot of our customers after they left. They didn't know it, and Mrs. Turner was a natural target. She obviously came from money with her expensive purses and her conceited ways. She'd try on a billion things, then buy maybe one shirt. That's something we retail employees do not appreciate since we gotta put all those clothes back on the rack. Sometimes I think she came in just to entertain her kid."

Trudy fiddled with an earring as she thought about what she was saying.

"Natalie really went to town on that Mrs. Turner sometimes."

"Went to town?" Sam asked.

Trudy giggled, then covered her mouth and took a moment to think before continuing.

"Yeah. I remember one time when Francine was at lunch and Mrs. Turner had just left, and it was just me and Natalie in the store. Natalie attacked that dressing room and started trying on all the clothes Mrs. Turner heaped in the corner. She twirled around and posed in front of the mirror and spoke with a fake British accent, pretending to be a queen, I guess. That Natalie could be a real hoot sometimes."

Sam sat sipping his coffee, the long day mostly behind him. After meeting with Roger Baker and Trudy Wilson, he'd come back to the office, caught up on his notes, and let what he'd learned so far gel in his mind.

The creek of his office door and whir of Casey's wheelchair interrupted his thoughts, a common, but not unpleasant, occurrence during Sam's in-office hours. He smiled as his blond, green-eyed assistant came through the door. The smile vanished, however, when Sam saw her face. Worry lines marred her usually cheerful face.

"What is it, Casey? Is Gus sick? Is Danny okay?"

Casey looked confused for a moment, and then shook herself.

"No, Sam. They're just fine, thanks. I've been doing some research…"

"And?" Sam asked.

"I'm still working on the Stewarts, but I did find another location where they lived through a former employer of Mr. Stewart. Before they were in Maryland, they lived in New York. I'm tracking that down now."

"Then what has you upset? I know you, dear. I know that look."

Casey's eyes traveled from the paper on her lap to Sam's face. She swallowed before talking.

"I think I may have some info about the neighbor, Albert Culver or Alfred Kulvert, as you discovered his alias was. It's not good news, I'm afraid…"

Sam sat across from Bob McCoy in Bob's office. He had called his friend yesterday afternoon to alert him about what Casey had found out.

"I'm afraid you've opened a can of worms with this Albert Culver/Alfred Kulvert thing," Bob said. "He hadn't been living in the neighborhood long enough for his background to catch up with him here, but we believe he is the same guy Casey found listed as a sex offender under Alfred Kulvert in the state of Utah. We're checking what she found against the FBI's list."

Sam shook his head. *This information is going be tough to share with Maggie*, he thought.

"Kulvert was caught with child pornography, and even though his lawyer successfully got a more serious charge of receiving pornography dropped, the judge gave him a few months in jail for the lesser offense of possession. We can't see that he has any molestation charges, but his sentence landed him on the public sex offenders lists…"

Sam sighed and ran one hand over his face.

"Pornography possession is a far cry from kidnapping, but I've got to let Maggie know. I can't believe he lived on the same street."

Bob's sigh matched Sam's.

"And I can't believe this fell through the cracks, though I guess it's possible the FBI checked it out. In our local department's defense, while we were spending our time following up on possible scenarios for Jenna's snatching, the guy moved out on us and became a non-issue. If he had been there a few more weeks, we may have come across his record here in the department. But the actual spelling of his name, Kulvert, and the switch from Albert to Alfred was just enough to bury the issue."

He leaned back in his chair and put his hands behind his head.

"I've alerted the FBI, in case they didn't make the connection, and I've filed for a person of interest APB to see if we can locate him. But it's been over two years. He's had some time to bury himself in the system again."

CHAPTER EIGHTEEN

MAGGIE SAT WITH A newspaper in her kitchen, but she couldn't seem to focus on the words. She was thinking about Jenna, and also about Sam.

The detective wasn't stereotypically handsome or particularly muscular. However, the fact she wondered exactly what his body looked like under his clothes bothered her. She hadn't thought about dating since her divorce. She was too wrapped up in Jenna's disappearance. Sam both distracted her from her obsession over her child and gave her a sounding board.

He was quiet, unassuming. He was a good listener. Maybe it was just that it had been so long since anyone or anything had taken her mind away from Jenna for a few hours, but it felt good to be with him…

He certainly was the polar opposite of Chad both in looks and personality.

"Maybe *that's* the attraction," Maggie muttered out loud. Conversation with Sam seemed natural. She felt completely without pressure to be smart or funny. For the few months Chad and she had dated before getting married, she found herself returning to how she was during her days of high school, when she had a reputation as slightly aloof, but mysterious, and intelligent and quick to come up with the right witty comment. It was a flirting mechanism and had charmed first Chad and then his business associates when they first married. But it grew tiring and false. By the time Jenna was a few months old, Maggie had begun to withdraw, leaving Chad to his business dealings while enjoying the domestic routine of motherhood. Even before the kidnapping, talking to her husband had become stiff and difficult, largely based on the day's events.

With Sam, she was just Maggie. She didn't have to *be* anything because he was just listening, figuring out the world alongside her.

Maggie got up from the kitchen table and went upstairs to her room to change her clothes, freshen her makeup, and comb her hair. It wasn't her usual routine to do this in the middle of the afternoon, unless she was already home and going back out to greet a client.

Sam arrived promptly at three and without asking, bent forward to plant a kiss on her cheek.

"*That* is against all the rules of being a detective," he said. "But you looked like you could use it."

She put her hand to her cheek and smiled. "To hell with rules indeed," she agreed. "Would you care for a glass of iced tea?"

The two adjourned to the kitchen. Maggie felt Sam's eyes on her as she stirred and poured two ice-cold beverages.

Sam sighed, breaking the lightness of his greeting. "I have some upsetting news, Maggie. But I think you should know what's going on."

She turned, handed him a glass, and then sat down before taking a long pull from her chilly drink. She set the glass down firmly.

"Okay, Sam. What is it?"

"It's about the guy who rented the house and had the van on the street—Albert Culver, the one who kind of gave you the creeps? We think it's an alias of Alfred Kulvert—spelled with a 'K' and a 'T' at the end. We connected the name to a registered sex offender in Utah."

Maggie's face paled and her frightened eyes connected with Sam's.

"Casey found Kulvert after an extensive search of national and state sex offender lists, though we haven't affirmed that he's the same man." He looked down at the table for moment, then found her eyes again as he added, "The officers that interviewed him back after Jenna was taken have now seen a mug shot from Utah authorities, and they think it's the same guy, though it's been too long to be positive. He'd also changed his appearance dramatically by the time he moved here. Authorities have put out an alert on him as a person of interest, but he hasn't been found yet. He never went back to the construction company he worked for when he came here."

Maggie's lips began to quiver, and she bit down on the bottom one. Sam reached across the table and took her hand.

"I know it's shocking news. However, think about this: he was charged with an extremely offensive, but not a major sex crime. He purchased child pornography over the Internet and police connected with that fact and raided his home. They found no other evidence of wrongdoing, nor was he ever connected with child molestation or another sex crime. He may have moved here under false pretenses, then moved again because of the kidnapping and the attention it was receiving."

Maggie's expression did not improve.

"He also had a solid alibi for where he was when Jenna was taken, as well as when the ransom was delivered. He was at work at a construction site across town from the mall."

A little color returned to her face.

"The police haven't written him off until they can locate him, question him, and check a few things. But I don't think, given the way it went down, that he was the kidnapper."

Sam smiled, trying to reassure her. He released her hand and gave the information a few moments to sink in.

"I feel confident enough that I'm pursuing other angles." He took a sip of tea and set his glass down.

"Now... what can you tell me about Nancy Maddox?"

Maggie's look turned to confusion. She repeated the name twice before exclaiming, "You mean Nancy Maddox from high school? The daughter of Charles Maddox?"

"That's the one."

"Well her father worked for my father's bank in the loan department, I think. He and my dad both climbed the corporate ladder to vice presidents. I remember something about Charles going to prison. I don't remember much about Nancy though."

"She was two years behind you in school. She and her mother moved away when she was a sophomore."

"I guess that's when Charles went to prison?"

"That's right. Did you know that it was your father who initially discovered the embezzlement that put him behind bars?"

Maggie was nodding her head. "I guess I knew that. But back then, I was so caught up in a teenager's world, I never paid much attention. I really never knew the family, although I do remember the mother. I think her name was Gladys?"

Maggie smiled wryly.

"That woman was quite full of herself and her husband's importance in the community. My mom used to joke about how snooty Gladys was, at least until her husband got caught dipping into the till. That much I do remember."

Her smile disappeared as she added, "I guess it had to have been a terrible blow to her pride to tumble so far so fast. What does this have to do with Jenna?"

"Probably nothing. But I've been told that the daughter had it out for you in high school."

The confusion returned to Maggie's face.

"*What?* If she disliked me, I never knew it. Of course, I probably wasn't paying much attention since she was a lowly sophomore when I was a senior."

Her brows furrowed and she pressed a forefinger to the side of her head, and then rubbed it as if she was getting a headache.

"That was a very long time ago, and I never heard anything about her after they moved away."

"I know. It's a long shot, but I'm working all angles," he said.

Sam stood and pulled Maggie to her feet. "Let's forget it all for now. I promised you a walk by the lake. We could both use the air."

Maggie smiled at Sam and cocked her head, glad to let the matter drop for now. She was barely a half-inch shorter than he was. She wondered briefly if his height bothered him. For her, it just made her eyes seek out the lips so close to hers and wonder what it would be like to kiss him.

Maggie shook off the thought and turned towards the door. But she tucked Sam's hand in the crook of her arm as they walked out together.

CHAPTER NINETEEN

SAM AND MAGGIE STROLLED leisurely, enjoying the sunshine of an unusually warm fall day, discussing the case, but mostly sharing tidbits about themselves.

When he left her at her house an hour later, she looked almost content—relaxed and no longer upset.

Sam drove directly to his house and entered the office instead of climbing the stairs to his living area. He needed to wrap his mind around something besides his feelings for his client.

Casey had gone home for the day and left a folder on his desk. That was usually a sign she'd found something, so Sam grabbed the folder and climbed the steps from his office to his home.

Taking a beer from the refrigerator, he sank down in his easy chair to read and to think. The folder contained clippings on the embezzlement, as well as background on Kulvert and more on the recent Allentown case. He glanced at the clock, saw that it was only 5:15, picked up his cell phone and dialed Chad Turner's office number. Chad was still there.

"Sure, I knew Nancy Maddox. She was a year or so younger than Maggie and I."

Chad chuckled.

"I'm not surprised Maggie doesn't remember her, though. They didn't exactly run around in the same crowd. Nancy never did much in school, wasn't in extracurricular activities. Got decent grades, if I remember right. I had a couple classes with her. And she did have a reputation."

"Oh?" Sam asked.

"The boys in school talked about her a lot because despite the fact she didn't have much of a face, she had a hot bod. She kinda had a crush on me. I hung out with her a bit, especially the couple of times Maggie and I broke up. After Nancy's dad got sent away to jail, though, no one saw much of her outside of school."

"Do you know what happened to her when she moved away?"

There was a pause before Chad replied.

"They moved an hour or so away—Columbia, Maryland, I think. Yeah, that's it. She kept in touch with me, or at least tried to. Called me and left messages, and emailed me, but I mostly ignored it."

Sam made no comment. He heard another chuckle.

"The summer we graduated, right after Maggie moved away, I did go and see her. We met up on the turnpike and…well. We *met up*, if you know what I mean. I was a free man. She was a willing partner."

Sam knew exactly what he meant and wondered why Chad felt he had to share this little tidbit.

"And you kept in touch after that?" Sam prodded.

"Her emails continued, and she liked to send me pictures of herself. I ignored the calls, though. She was a little too clingy for my taste. Fortunately for me, it all became a non-issue when the family moved on to some other place. Ohio, I think. I don't know exactly where, and I never heard from her again."

"And when you were all still in school, did you get the feeling Nancy disliked Maggie?"

"She said a few nasty things about Maggie. I figured it was jealousy talking. What can I say?"

Sam thanked him and disconnected. Putting the telephone back in its charge base, he went downstairs again, rummaged through his drawer for file cards, grabbed his white-board and carried it back up to his apartment. After nibbling and never quite tasting a frozen dinner, he washed his dishes and went back to whiteboard and file cards. He sat in his chair and ran the facts through his head so many times that he fell asleep.

Sam woke to a slightly stiff neck and sun-shine peeking through his living room win-dow. He'd slept through the night in his chair, which wasn't an unusual situation when he was working on a puzzle.

Sam decided he needed more information about high school and that the quickest place to get it was from the woman most willing to share it: Dottie Alstead.

Dottie greeted Sam with the eagerness of a puppy left too long alone in the house. She offered him coffee, then coffee cake, and when Sam had both in hand, she invited him to sit on the porch.

Dottie herself settled into a wooden rock-ing chair where Sam imagined she spent a lot of time—observing neighbors on her street com-ing and going.

"Yes, of course, I remember details about the scandal. I was a customer at the bank and also got the inside scoop from one of the tellers, who was my friend," she said. "Mr. Maddox went to prison, I believe, and the family moved to Maryland."

"According to Chad, the family then moved to Ohio. Would you happen to know where?"

The sly look on Dottie's face caught Sam's attention.

"I'm not surprised Chad would know where Nancy was after she left here."

"Why would you think that?" Sam asked.

She paused, her mug almost to her lips. Then, without drinking, she set it down on a porch table and leaned forward.

"Poor dear Maggie never knew this, but Chad and that Nancy girl had a little side action going in high school."

"You mean they were having a sexual relationship while Nancy still lived here?" Sam prodded.

Dottie sat back and clasped her hands together.

"Well, no one knew for sure. But I caught them once beneath the bleachers."

"You caught them in the act?"

"Well, they weren't actually *doing* it, but they may as well have been."

"Do you think Maggie knew this?"

"Oh, no. Probably not. She kinda lived in her own little world sometimes. Still does, really. And like I said, she didn't have that many girlfriends. It was generally accepted though, among those of us who paid *attention* to such goings on."

"I thought you said Chad had eyes only for Maggie?" Sam asked.

"Chad was one of those guys who managed to keep the cool girl and the…easy girl at the same time," she said.

Sam wondered why there was a note of admiration in her voice. He set his own mug down for the next question.

"Do you think Chad and Nancy kept in touch?"

Dottie looked towards Maggie's house, then lowered her voice as if Maggie might hear.

"Chad took that final break up pretty hard. Maggie gave him back his ring just two weeks before the prom. She went with another boy. Chad showed up drunk at the prom. I was there with my Harold, of course, God rest his soul. Chad and Harold were friends, so Chad sat at our table and did a little bragging. That's when I learned for sure that he and Nancy had been *doing* it."

"Poor Maggie," Dottie added. Sam detected

no real pity in her voice. After a few more questions, he stood, thanked Dottie for the coffee and turned to walk down the porch steps.

"Youngstown," Dottie said. Sam turned back, a question in his eyes.

"I believe the family went to Youngstown, Ohio after they left Maryland."

Maggie threw open her front door and greeted Sam warmly as he stepped onto her porch. "I saw you a few minutes ago," she said. "I guess you were going to talk to Dottie again?"

Sam looked towards Dottie's porch. The neighborhood gossip sat finishing her coffee and watching her kingdom. She lifted a hand to wave at Maggie.

"That's right. I just had a few questions for her." He turned back towards Maggie and stepped inside, out of Dottie's sight.

Maggie, who was dressed today in a soft beige blouse and jeans, a scarf tied round her head, brought her hand up to the wrap.

"Sorry. I wasn't prepared for company. I have a couple days off, and I'm practicing my domestic skills." She stepped back from Sam and gestured to the kitchen.

"Can I offer you some coffee?"

"No, thanks. I just had a cup with your neighbor." But Sam followed her down the hallway into the kitchen, where one cupboard's contents were sprawled on the counter.

"I'm doing a little spring cleaning," she explained.

"I'm sorry to interrupt. I didn't intend to stop by, but I was in the neighborhood…" Sam began.

Maggie turned toward him, and once again, he was wowed by her eyes.

"Sam, you don't need an excuse. I'm glad you stopped."

Sam shook his head slowly and decided to be honest.

"To tell you the truth, I had every intention of avoiding you this morning. I really did come to talk to Dottie, but my feet seem drawn to this house."

Maggie sighed deeply. "It's not quite right, is it?" She walked up close to Sam and rested a palm on the side of his face. "We're getting too close, and I'm just a client."

Sam rested his own hand on the back of hers.

"It goes against the rules, yes. I've never been too good with the rules."

They stood that way for a few moments, drawn to each other and fighting the impulse to collide. Sam was the first to gain control. He dropped his hand. She dropped hers.

"It's early. Too early, probably, to feel this

way. Hopefully, we can explore this at some point. That is, if you're interested in doing so. For now, we'll focus on what we need to do to find Jenna." He stepped back. "But know this: I want more."

"Understood," Maggie replied.

Sam grinned. "Now how about some lunch since I'm here?"

Maggie turned away, but didn't seem upset. She simply started putting things back in her cupboard.

"And maybe you want to ride along with me tomorrow?" Sam asked. Maggie turned back to him, her eyebrows raised.

"I've got work to do; you're part of that work," Sam explained. "Why not ride along and spend some time with me?"

"And just where will be going, Detective Osborne?" she teased.

"York, Pennsylvania, then Columbia, Maryland, if you have the time. I need to find where Natalie Collins lived in York, and if anyone knows much about her."

"Natalie Collins? The store clerk?"

"The store clerk working when Jenna went missing."

"What are you looking for?" Maggie asked, clearly intrigued. "I'm sure the police interviewed her."

"Of course they did. And they may have poked around on her background. But there is usually a lot more to dig up than the standard police follow-up reveals. I contacted the place where Natalie lived and want to talk to her landlord to get a feel for her life away from the store."

"And Columbia?" Maggie asked. She was finished with the cupboard and took off the kerchief, smoothing her hair with her hands.

"I want to pay a visit to the neighborhood in Columbia where the Maddox family went after Lancaster," Sam said.

"So you don't feel the Maddox family is ancient history?" Maggie found her purse and was brushing her hair. She returned brush to purse and put the bag on her shoulder.

"There is no such thing as ancient when it comes to something like this," Sam said. He draped his arm around Maggie's shoulders. The two left to grab a bite.

When Sam got back to the office later that night, he left a note for Casey to read in the morning:

See what you can find out about the Maddox family: father Charles, wife Gladys and children Nancy and Chuck—after they moved to Youngstown, Ohio.

CHAPTER TWENTY

THE NEXT MORNING, AFTER picking up a coffee at a drive-through window, Sam and Maggie rode in silence towards York, each lost in their individual thoughts. Suddenly, Maggie turned towards Sam.

"You know a lot about me and my past and my current woes. I need to know more about Sam."

He chuckled.

"Okay, 'detective' Turner, fire away."

"Tell me more about your marriage."

Sam groaned and kept his eyes on the road as he gave her the staccato version.

"Police detective who works too many hours. Wife who feels ignored. Wife who doesn't work and loves to go out at night. Husband who is tired after a grueling day of doing police work and has no desire to go anywhere. Husband who ignores the fact she 'goes out' more and more frequently and not realizing exactly what that meant, which was sometimes other men."

His expression sobered.

"We were headed for divorce before it became a reality, then Davie came along, Barbara settled down a little, and we both enjoyed parenthood. Unfortunately, the glue of a child didn't hold our family together very well and the whole thing came crashing down after Davie disappeared. It wasn't a very nice divorce."

"And what about your family. Are your mother and father still alive? Do you have siblings?"

"Mom passed away when I was just a teenager. Dad and I had a long and good relationship. He was a policeman. But he's been gone about ten years. I miss him like hell and started this whole detective business based on the money he left me. He would have been pleased to know I was doing what I want with my life."

Sam was silent, but only for a minute. The corners of his mouth turned up.

"And I have one bossy sister in Boston who is *still* trying to set me up with women. I have a pretty good relationship with her husband

and their two darling kids, but I don't see them enough."

He took his eyes off the road, and sought out Maggie's. "That's the Cliff notes version. More to come later. That's probably more than I've shared with anyone in a while, but I have the distinct impression you'll drag details out of me later, anyway."

Maggie laughed.

"Okay, now my turn, Ms. Maggie Turner. Just one question: *Chad?*"

Maggie laughed louder. Then she sobered enough to collect her thoughts.

"He can be a real charmer when he wants to be. I fell for it in high school, and I fell for it 15 years later when I moved back to town. He'd already been married once for a pretty short amount of time, and maybe that should have told me something. I wasn't ready to pay attention. It was a vulnerable time in my life. I was returning to the town I grew up in after a failed attempt at making it in the big city of New York."

She was staring hard out the window, and then turned her head back to Sam.

"Well, actually I did *make* it professionally. I worked for a big ad firm—I studied marketing in school. And I made a pretty good salary in the big city, but I was miserable the whole time

I was there. I don't get along that well with the city life. I am a lot happier selling real estate in a small town, though I've only been doing this five or six years."

Sam took his eyes from the road long enough for a quick smile. He didn't say anything.

Maggie's eyes returned to the road.

"Pretty quickly after I came back, I let Chad's charm work for about six months—making me feel good and safe and back in the old nest where I grew up. I think I just really needed it.

"But he was a busy man, and we didn't really see each other that often. After I found out I was pregnant with Jenna, I guess I envisioned the small town life, though my vision included working. Chad, on the other hand, envisioned a country club wife at home, someone who was an extension of his own life. I had to fight tooth and nail just to go back to real estate school and get my license. He would have preferred a woman who only hung on his arm at social affairs and changed his baby girl's diapers for a living."

Sam's smile was crooked; his eyes remained on the road.

"It's funny, but I can see you as both the woman wearing a fancy suit to deal with difficult clients and at home, wrinkling your nose over baby poop."

They laughed in unison at the comment.

Maggie and Sam arrived at their destination, a brick apartment building in York on a street bordering an industrial park.

"I have an appointment with the manager of this apartment building—Natalie's last address."

They climbed a set of concrete, pock-marked steps, rang the buzzer to the building and, after several minutes and a verbal identification through the intercom, were greeted by a round man with a bald head, sweating armpits, and a huge, welcoming grin.

"Yeah, I remember Natalie," the man said when they were seated in a small office in a cramped apartment that smelled slightly of kitty litter.

"She was a chatterbox. Always talking about where she and that husband were going to go—showed me brochures a couple times of tropical this and beach-town that. Big dreams that lady, 'specially since I knew she worked in a mall with occasional waitress jobs when she needed extra cash."

"What was the husband like?" Sam asked.

"Big mean-looking dude. I suppose women who like the brawny type would think him handsome. The look on his face, however, was dangerous. Never said a whole lot to anyone."

"Did they move in, then move out together then?" Sam asked.

The man tilted his head to think.

"Come to think of it, I'm not even sure they were together when she left. I didn't see him for a good maybe three or four weeks before she packed up and was gone. Maybe he just got tired of the old chatterbox."

"Any idea where either of them moved?"

"No, and they left the apartment a wreck. Had to hire a clean-up lady. It was a furnished apartment, so the furniture stayed. Their rent was paid up, so I didn't pursue back rent, though they lost the deposit. It took us a couple of afternoons to clean out the trash."

"So they never talked about where they were headed?" Sam prodded.

"I assumed they finally took one of those grand trips, either together or separately. Just got sick of their lives, maybe. Can't say I haven't wanted to do that myself."

Suddenly he cocked his head. "I did keep a box of papers from the clean-up. I was hoping, at the time, that something in there might help me track them down and get them to pay for the mess. But to tell you the truth, there was no damage, just a lot of cleaning, so it wasn't worth it."

"I don't suppose you still have that box?" Sam asked. He was amazed when the manager got up, went into another room, and came back with a shoebox.

"I flipped through here at one point, but it's mostly just unopened mail. You may as well take this," he continued. "I know I'll never get around to doing anything with it."

Sam thanked him and took the box. He and Maggie sat in the car rifling through the contents, hoping for a clue. After twenty minutes, Sam triumphantly held up a letter.

"You have something?" Maggie asked.

"Maybe. It's a letter confirming a cottage rental in St. Mary's Creek, Ohio addressed to John Collins. But it's around the time of the kidnapping. If they went on a grand vacation, I don't think it would have been to Ohio."

Maggie grabbed the letter.

"This has to mean *some*thing, Sam. Doesn't it? Do you think the two things are related?"

"We'll check it out," Sam promised. He started the engine, backed the car out of its parking space and headed it towards Maryland.

"And where are we going now, Detective Osborne?" Maggie asked.

Sam smiled. "I want to visit the school where Nancy Maddox went after she left Lancaster. I made an appointment with the principal at Columbia High School in Maryland."

"Well, that's good," she said chuckling. "I thought maybe you were heading all the way to

St. Mary's, Ohio. I'm about ready to, to tell you the truth. It seems like a good lead."

"I'll let you know if I decide to make that trip," Sam replied. He looked over at her briefly, and then returned his eyes to the road.

After ten minutes of relaxed silence, Maggie spoke. She had been staring out her window again lost in her past.

"There was a short period in our marriage that was actually good. It was just after Jenna was born. Suddenly, we had this tiny being we shared a love for. She was a topic of conversation, a daily source of wonder. I believe Chad loves Jenna as much as I do. At least, in spirit. He's just not the kind of man where that love translates into patience. As soon as Jenna was old enough to be under foot, he started spending more and more time away from home. He couldn't stand what he called her 'prattle' and her constant demands to play Crazy Eights or have a tea party. But I know he loves her. That's why I can't believe he's given up looking for her."

Sam took his eyes off the road long enough to glance her way again.

"I understand what you're saying. Jenna gave meaning to your lives. That's what Davie did to mine. My marriage never meant that much. I realize that now; but I loved my little boy."

Maggie turned to Sam then, her eyes glistening with tears.

"When Jenna was taken from us, I couldn't bear to even look at Chad. He didn't know how to give comfort—only demand it of me, and everyone else. He was angry with me, angry at the police, angry at the FBI. I was just devastated and in need of some kind words. We didn't go through our pain together, and I sometimes felt like he was competing for the pity and attention."

Maggie sighed, closed her eyes and turned forward to lean back against her seat.

The traveling companions arrived an hour and a half later at a red brick building. They waited inside the school office complex several minutes before the lanky form of Principal Jim Brown came out of his personal office.

"Sam Osborne?" he asked as he approached their chairs.

Sam introduced Maggie without explaining who she was, and the three went into the principal's office. Jim sat behind an enormous desk while Maggie and Sam sat side by side in front of the desk in stiff, wooden chairs. Jim Brown's kind eyes contrasted sharply with the size of his desk and stiffness of the chairs.

"Now what can I do for you?" he asked in a deep voice.

"We are looking into the whereabouts of a 1990 graduate—Nancy Maddox. I know that was a long time ago, but we're wondering if her past will lead us to her present."

"Ah," he signed as he leaned back. "Sadly, we always remember the students who gave us problems. It's the obedient kids who don't get into hot water that we sometimes forget."

Sam explained what they were investigating, and the principal rose from his chair and walked over to a long row of file cabinets that lined one wall. When he returned to his chair, he held one folder in his hand.

"Nancy transferred here from Lancaster at the beginning of her junior year and begin a two-year pattern of behavior problems. Nothing major, but she often ended up in my office or in counseling."

He looked up from studying the papers.

"We knew that her father was in prison, and though the information was supposed to be confidential, someone in the student body found out, and I'm afraid they made her life hard after that. Consequently, she fought back by acting up whenever she got the opportunity. It seemed like she was always in trouble—with us here at the school, and, several times that we know of, with the police, though I don't believe she was ever arrested.

They visited us several times to ask questions about her."

"Is there an address in that file on where she went after graduation?" Sam asked.

Jim looked from Sam to Maggie, and then rose.

"I cannot release the official file to you without a legal request. However, I do have my own personal notes on Nancy—I liked to keep track of each student—and I'll have my secretary copy those, as well as her school picture, along with that address."

When he returned to the office, Jim handed a few sheets of paper to Sam, who stuck them in the portfolio he always carried with him. The three said their goodbyes and Maggie and Sam were once again in the car.

They sat for a few moments lost in their own thoughts before Sam started the car and headed for home.

"It must have been hard on her to have a father in prison," Maggie said softly. She was staring out the window again. "I guess I never gave that much thought. I guess she could have resented the fact my father was responsible for hers being in jail."

After a few minutes, her focus returned to the inside of the car, and she opened Sam's portfolio and rifled through the papers Jim had given them. Her eyes stopped when they got to a sheet with a school photo.

As she stared at Nancy's picture, her eyes widened and her breathing became shallow.

"Oh, my God!"

CHAPTER TWENTY-ONE

JOHN WATCHED HIS WIFE as she approached their side-by-side beach chairs. He never grew bored looking at her curves. She was not a classically beautiful woman, but her poise and her body turned many men's heads, and she kept that body in shape with swimming and, when they'd been able to afford it, the gym.

John returned to his magazine. He wasn't always happy with the way she behaved, and he'd never understood the way she thought. But she was his—all his. She'd proven her loyalty over and over again.

No one who passed by him could see his grin behind the magazine.

As far as the bedroom, he'd never had a

better time. She was always hot and ready for him, and she rarely said 'no.' She was also very aware of the effect she had on him, and he liked the fact she used it to get what she wanted.

John glanced at her as she seductively ran her own suntan lotion-laden hands over her curves, raising one hand above her head to get the underside of an arm. The movement made her breasts plump outward. Her long, blond hair fell in waves around those breasts and her shoulders. He was glad she'd returned to blond. He'd hated her with dark hair, even if it was closer to her natural color.

Though John's groin tightened, he closed his eyes to feign sleep and suggest to her he might be bored. He knew she'd play the game.

John knew he wasn't in love, in the romantic way the books and movies portrayed, or even anywhere near what he'd felt for Kate. He certainly wouldn't give his own life to save his wife's. She was wild, she was selfish, and she was too unconnected to anything but her own needs to engender feelings of tenderness or sentimentality—if he'd had any to give in the first place. He'd had that kind of "love" exactly one time in his life, and it had only caused him pain. He had no need or desire for anything more than what he had now.

Natalie stood then, and he felt her shadow fall across his face. He opened his eyes.

Taking off her sun hat, she smiled and said, "I wish you'd come in the water with me. It's wonderfully refreshing."

She stretched her long limbs and plopped down at the bottom of his lounge chair. "You do look good enough to eat," she teased, leaning over like she was going to kiss him. Instead, she playfully nibbled on his neck.

"I'm napping here in paradise, dear. It's my definition of relaxing."

Natalie smiled again and reached over to stroke his chest with her long fingers. Those fingers began to move southward.

"Not here, my dear," John said, his breath quickening. "Shall we retire to the cabin?"

"We need to talk."

But John was already getting up, anxious to get on with the afternoon.

"Okay, we'll talk afterwards."

He laughed and pulled her out of the chair. Hand-in-hand, they walked back to their little slice of paradise, touching each other with their free hands along the way.

Their lovemaking was quick, but intense, leaving clothes strewn about the cabin, bruises on their bodies and both of them gasping for breath, waiting for their hearts to still so they could try it again at a more leisurely pace.

Before they could begin again, Natalie spoke.

"We're almost out of money, John. We have to do something."

Her voice was almost a whisper—just enough to bring John back to Earth too abruptly.

He sighed and Natalie turned her head, and then her body towards him. She laid one hand on his stomach, just above the hair that covered his sex.

"I don't want this to end, do you?" she purred and stroked.

"Of course not."

"Then we have to get some more money. What about another kidnapping?"

"No!" John said. He flung both hands above his head on the pillow.

Natalie sat up suddenly, anger written on her face.

"And why not, pray tell. It certainly went well the last time."

"No more kidnappings," John said more firmly. "They're too public. Too unpredictable."

Natalie turned to look down at him.

"John, dear. We pulled the last one off beautifully. No one can tie us to any of it. We ended up here in this lovely place. *Why in the world* wouldn't we do what we've found out we're good at?"

John was silent.

"Oh, good lord. Don't tell me it's because

you're squeamish about killing kids? What is the damn difference? They're just littler people."

He stared at the ceiling, still silent.

"You've killed plenty of bigger brats in your time."

John got up and put on his clothes, not answering Natalie, who began to worry. John began straightening up the room, which worried her further.

She just sat there thinking, her perfect round breasts now covered by her arms; the sheet pulled around her middle.

"Johnny. Dearest. I know it isn't easy. But I have an idea this time that doesn't involve killing at all. Unless someone gets in our way of course."

John stopped what he was doing long enough to glance in her direction.

She grinned and patted the bed beside her, inviting him to sit.

"I was going to save this as a surprise. But I've been talking to the Carlsons. You know how close I've gotten to Glenda. Did you know they can't have kids? All that money, and what do they want? Some little guy to spend it all on. It's amazing really."

John was pretty sure the Carlsons couldn't have kids for more than biological reasons. Like John and Natalie, he suspected there was much more to their story than what they told the wealthy patrons of the establishment where they were staying. "Carlson" probably wasn't even their name. John didn't know the full story, but he'd talked to Jim Carlson enough to know they could not go back to the United States.

"Glenda went on and on one night about how much she wanted a kid, and I sort of alluded to the fact we had connections to an adoption place that wasn't on the books. I made up some story about us looking into adopting."

Natalie patted the bed again.

"Johnny, she got all excited and...well. She said they'd pay half a million for a kid!"

John finally sat on the bed next to her, but instead of excitement, his face looked tired.

"I can't do it, Natalie."

"Why-ever the hell *not*! I thought you'd be pleased with this simple plan. We just take a young kid and wham. Half a million! And you don't have to hurt the child except maybe to drug him long enough to get him here."

John said nothing. More minutes ticked by. Suddenly, Natalie sprang out of bed, pulling the sheet with her and pacing. She stopped in front of John.

In a voice edged with cold steel, she repeated, "What has you so bothered by this?

You listened to me the last couple times I suggested something. What the hell is the matter now?"

After several more moments, John's defeated face rose and his eyes sought hers.

"Things didn't exactly go as well as you thought with the last kidnapping," John said.

Natalie cocked her head and stood waiting for more, her chest rising and falling, her hands still clutching the sheet.

"I had some trouble with the killing."

"What do you mean by *trouble*?" Her glare was penetrating John's very skull.

"You mean trouble as in someone saw you? Trouble as in you didn't dispose of the body? Trouble as in the kid wouldn't *die* for a while?"

John said nothing. His head dropped into his hands.

"Tell me you don't mean you didn't get rid of the evidence!"

When he still did not speak, Natalie lost it completely. The sheet dropped to the floor because she was busy pummeling him with her fists.

"How dare you endanger us like this. It was one simple killing. You idiot. You imbecile. You moron. One simple damn step and you couldn't DO it. You've ruined the whole thing. How could you do this?"

Instead of reacting, John sat taking it. He'd been the source of her temper tantrums enough times to know she'd wear herself out. She couldn't really hurt him—he was too big. After five minutes of yelling and hitting, Natalie suddenly stopped, turned and sat down beside him on the bed.

"Geez, I had it all set up. The Carlsons agreed to live out of the country in one of their foreign houses. No one would be able to trace where the child went. We would be set for years with five hundred thousand. Instead, we're likely to be arrested if we go back to the States. I'm sure the kid has talked by now. What the hell did you do?"

"Let me think, Nat. Let me think." John got up and began his own pacing. Natalie was quiet. She knew that pacing was a good thing. It meant he was looking for a solution.

After five minutes, John picked up the discarded sheet and covered Natalie, sat beside her and began to talk.

"I don't think we're in any danger. I took the kid to my brother's."

"The Amish brother? Really? Why would you go to him?"

"Because I knew the child would be raised behind a wall of silence. I also knew that if Eli thought the kid was mine, he'd agree to it. And

I knew that the community would accept that Eli and Rebecca were raising a relative from an 'English' family."

Natalie began to nod her head. "I have to admit, if you were looking for a solution that didn't involve killing, that was a good one."

John was surprised she was taking it so well. But Natalie was nodding her head again.

"No one would ever think of looking among the Amish, and the Amish wouldn't likely see the TV reports of a missing child if it wasn't a local thing."

Her head stopped nodding.

"Do you really think you can trust this brother who you haven't seen in years to keep this a secret somehow? And what about the kid?"

"I know my brother and Rebecca. I'm sure they found a way to explain to the society who the child was. If the kid had managed to turn me in, we would have heard a long time ago. Believe me, I've monitored every newspaper and news channel. It just didn't happen. No one has reported a strange kid popping up in that community."

John reached over and took Natalie's hand.

"Babe, I am so relieved to tell you all this. I don't know why I could not do what we planned. I've never hesitated before. Why are you taking this so well?"

Natalie was grinning slyly.

"Because, my dear, you've prepared us for stage two. It's perfect. We have the Carlson's child. Now all we have to do is get our meal ticket back from your brother."

CHAPTER TWENTY-TWO

Benjy sat on an old log, his drawing pad and colored pencils working fervently. He was drawing a picture of a bird for Mother, fervently hoping it would bring another smile to the usually stern face. Just last week, he'd shyly left a pretty, multi-colored scene of barn and fields, crops and flowers on Mother's sewing table with his name and a big red heart scribbled at the bottom. Mother had hugged him tightly when she'd picked him up at school, something she rarely did. Benjy was confused at first, until he'd remembered leaving her the picture.

He never saw the picture again, but he knew, in his heart, it had made her happy, just as he knew she wouldn't display the gift because

Father would not approve of a boy who spent too much time drawing silly pictures.

The picture he was drawing now was beginning to look just right. The beak and the feathers were fun to draw, but the eyes had given him much trouble. As he erased them yet again, he frowned and picked up a purple pencil.

His concentration was broken by the sound of other children shouting and laughing. He lifted his head and watched the game of volleyball going on in the churchyard. Church was over and the adults were turning the church benches into tables to serve fried chicken and corn and the rest of the good bounty that followed meeting time.

Benjy's mouth watered just thinking about it, but he knew it would be many minutes before the children were called to eat. The oldest of the church members would eat first, followed by young couples with children. Benjy's Mother and Father would eat in separate rooms, and Benjy would go with Father. Then the family would be among the first to leave for home.

Benjy knew he should finish what he was doing and go to join the other children so that Father and Mother would find him playing, not drawing. However, his best friends, Joshua and Hannah, were home sick with their family, so he didn't really want to play. Benjy liked all of the children, and no one was mean to him. But he knew he was different than them, and it kept him from making many friends. He had secrets to keep, people to protect. He had to have patience, and like the good book said, he had to have love for everyone. He didn't belong in this world, but it was not a bad place to be. The people were kind and not boastful; good Christian people who, like him, worked hard and took care of their families.

Benjy sighed. He rested his back against the tree and looked at the fluffy clouds. It was a pretty day, and God had provided another good week of health for his family and food for the table. Mother and Father were safe. And today, there were treats to come and no work, and for that, he thanked God. He picked up his purple pencil and bent to his work.

CHAPTER TWENTY-THREE

MAGGIE WAS BREATHING IN short gasps. Her hand grasping the picture began to shake.

"What's the matter? Are you okay?" Sam cried. His eyes left the road long enough to study her face, and then followed her troubled eyes to the face in the picture.

"They're the same!" Maggie gasped. "Nancy Maddox is Natalie Collins."

Sam's eyes returned to the road. "I suspected that might be the case, Maggie."

Maggie's head whipped around to stare at Sam. "You *suspected*? You aren't surprised? You never said a word about this. I can't believe you knew."

Sam's face was calm. "I didn't know. I had no photo of Natalie. We haven't been able to track her down except for that last place she lived. I've been working that angle, however, because Natalie lied on her application about other things such as where she worked last. Even the police suspected Natalie Collins because she seemed to drop off the face of the Earth. But they didn't make the connection with Nancy. You just did."

Maggie's eyes returned to the picture, but it suddenly felt wrong in her hands. She slipped it back into the folder.

Sam continued. "I've also been working the angle that Nancy Maddox had something to do with this kidnapping," Sam explained. "The ransom was the exact amount her father embezzled and went to jail for."

Maggie was nodding her head.

"I also felt, however, that the kidnapper wanted more from you than money. You live in a pretty well off community with lots of other children and people far more wealthy than you and Chad. There had to be a reason Jenna was selected."

Sam drove the car into a small cul de sac and turned off the ignition. He took the folder from her lap and opened it again to pull out the picture.

"At the same time, it was also just enough that you and Chad could realistically raise it quickly enough for a ransom drop. The person had to have known that. Nancy Maddox was supposedly long gone from this area. Natalie, however, was a local."

He looked down at the picture.

"Does she look very different then from this picture in high school?" He turned the picture towards Maggie. Despite her aversion to having to look at Nancy's face, Maggie took it from him to study again. "Yes, very much so. I mean Natalie's hair was dark, almost black as I remember."

Maggie touched a forefinger to the face in the picture.

"I also think Nancy had cosmetic surgery. She always had a shapely body as I recall, but she would never have been called pretty. Her features were blunt, her nose large; her ears pretty big too. When I think of Natalie, I think attractive, despite too much makeup. I never connected the two, probably because I didn't see Natalie, except a few times in the store, and I wasn't really *looking* if you know what I mean. I was busy shopping. And I guess I never was around Nancy Maddox much in high school, either. She was two years younger and kind of crude, as I recall. At least that's how my teen-age-self thought of her." Her eyes rose from the picture. "God, she must really have thought I was full of myself not to have recognized her in the store."

Tears pooled in her eyes, but she blinked rapidly to clear them away. "I hardly knew her —why did she hate me so?"

She turned glistening eyes to Sam.

"Was it because of her father going to jail and what my father did to facilitate that? Why would she hold it against me? How could she hate me so much after all this time that she'd take the one thing most precious to me?"

Sam put his arm around her and drew her close to his solid warmth. "I don't know. There's often more than one motive for a crime like this. She may have planned the whole kidnapping after having met you again in the store. She may have resented the fact you didn't recognize her, or maybe the fact you married Chad set off something. More than one person told me Chad and Nancy saw each other in high school as well as the year after you broke up. Maybe she was getting back at Chad, too. It could have been any of those reasons… or all of them."

Maggie buried her face in Sam's chest for a few moments, relishing the strength she felt there. When she finally withdrew and brought her eyes back up to Sam's face, he felt a jolt of physical pain from the grief he read on her face.

"I cannot believe I was such an idiot. My

stupidity may have cost me...Sam, do you think she killed Jenna?"

Sam tucked a stray curl behind one of her ears.

"I don't think we have any idea who Nancy Maddox turned into when she left Lancaster and started her life as Natalie. Being a jealous or angry teenager doesn't mean she became a killer. It doesn't do us any good to speculate. It will do us a lot more good to keep looking for the truth."

He started the car back up and drove for a few minutes.

"I think we need to track down who 'Natalie' is and where she is." He glanced at Maggie quickly.

"If you're up to it and you can get away, do you want to take a trip to Ohio next week? The drive might do us both some good—clear our heads and give us some thinking and talking time. I'm having Casey and her husband Danny check on a bunch of things here, including following up on the Allentown case. But we need to take a stab at something deeper from your past. The FBI and the police poked around in a lot of areas, but we've already found some things they couldn't by simply visiting Nancy's past."

Maggie was nodding her head. She reached over and touched Sam on the arm.

"Why Ohio?"

Sam glanced at the hand on his arm and smiled. He liked it when she touched him.

"The Maddox family ended up there. I want to check out Nancy's old neighborhood, which is about four-and-a-half hours away from here in Youngstown, then maybe go on to that place where the cottage is—St. Mary's—and see what the connection to Natalie and John Collins might be."

Maggie tilted her head to think for just a moment, and then raised the back of her hand to Sam's cheek.

"Sounds like a plan, Sam. No matter what we find, thank you for including me in all this. I've lived so long in limbo. It just feels good to be moving forward and working on something concrete."

She smiled and let her hand trail down Sam's cheek.

"I'll clear my schedule early next week," she said.

Chapter Twenty-Four

Sam turned off the lights in his office and climbed wearily up the stairs to his personal apartment. He settled in front of the television, but as usual, there was nothing he felt like watching so after 10 minutes of flipping through the channels, he gave up, fixed and ate a sandwich in the kitchen, then retreated to his bedroom.

He hated taking sleeping pills, but he could feel his mind bouncing from Jenna and the case to Maggie and back again.

Sam sighed, popped a pill and crawled into bed.

He couldn't figure out why he felt like he'd known Maggie forever—like she was a friend he'd grown up with. Meeting her and taking on this case had changed the structure of his life somehow. He was not the same man he'd been before that first visit with Maggie. He knew the relationship was challenged by the reality that she was a client. What would happen to them if he could not find Jenna or if he discovered that Jenna had been killed?

Sam turned over and slugged his pillow a couple of times, trying to ease the ache in his neck by giving it more support.

The whys and ifs don't really matter, and even if I could find answers to those questions, it doesn't change what I feel, he thought.

Her soft lips, her feathery hair, those astonishing eyes, that soft skin he longed to explore. Her quick and quiet intelligence, her bravery in the face of something as tragic as losing a child, he wanted Maggie both emotionally and physically, and he knew she was already part of him—at least for now.

Sam gave up and rose from his bed. He returned to his chair, opened a magazine, read a few paragraphs, absorbed none of the meaning of the words, and laid the booklet down in his lap. Finally, he fell asleep.

Sam and his son Davie were walking hand in hand down a long dirt road lined on both sides by tall stalks of corn. Sam knew this wasn't real; it was just in his head—a fond wish. But he didn't care. He felt blessed to be in this moment.

Davie, who had been swinging Sam's hand, suddenly tugged on it several times. "Daddy, daddy a farmhouse. And a real barn. Do you think they have cows? Can we go visit?"

Sam glanced over where Davie was pointing.

He didn't like what he saw. The farmhouse was old and worn, the porch beams looked like they were barely holding up the overhang. The barn looked in better structural shape, but it was devoid of paint, grey wood that stretched towards the sky with a roof so high he couldn't see the top. Sam saw no people around and was about to tell Davie "no," when he felt the boy let go of his hand. Without asking further permission, Davie began to run towards the buildings.

"Davie, stop, we don't know whose property this is!"

Davie ignored him and continued to run, leaving a cloud of dust in his wake. The dust rose to choke Sam, who coughed and began waving his arms in an attempt to calm the cloud enough to find where Davie had headed. All he could see was the underside of the tall barn's roof. He moved toward that sight guessing Davie would seek out the cows first.

Sam made his way to barn where he noticed

the door was slightly ajar. Davie must have already entered. He put shoulder to door and shoved until the opening was wide enough to let him in. Once inside, he was out of the dust, but the lighting was so low all Sam could make out was the floor, which was illuminated from the door opening and dotted with light spots that must have come from holes in the roof.

"Davie, son. Where are you?" His call echoed in the large room and Sam's eyes began to adjust. He saw no animals, no stalls. Only stacks and stacks of bound hay piled as high as his head in rows. He moved down one of those rows, calling Davie's name over and over.

He heard only a giggle in reply.

"Davie, is that you?"

He came to the end of a row of stacked hay and his eye caught movement down another of those rows.

He turned in that direction and found himself facing a second long row of stacked bales that was even higher than the last.

Sam became frantic. He had to find his boy. He put his hand on the hay walls and began to move quickly down that row. It ended suddenly and Sam almost fell into a large chamber at the end of the row.

"Davie, boy, where are you?" he said again.

"Daddy, come get me daddy. I'm up here."

Sam looked high into the chamber and through the light coming from the roof holes, he could just make out the outline of a hayloft. He moved forward and almost stumbled over a ladder resting on the floor. It had probably led up to the loft. Davie must have climbed into the loft, then lost the ladder.

"Son, I'm coming to get you. Hold still."

He picked up the rickety ladder and wondered that it had held together under the weight of his son. He had to use it himself to try to reach his boy. Would it hold?

"Davie, are you up there? Show me your face so I know where you are," Sam shouted upwards.

"No, silly. You know you can't find me. I'm not really here." He heard the voice coming from the loft, but it didn't sound like his son.

"Davie, are you up there? Show yourself," he called up the ladder.

A head popped up from the loft floor and looked over the edge. But instead of Davie, Sam saw Jenna Turner staring down at him.

The jarring ring Sam had chosen for his cell phone woke him. He shuddered away the rest of the dream and leaned over onto the little table he kept by his chair to pick up his cell. He passed a hand over his face to clear the cobwebs.

"Detective Sam Osborne?" a voice said.

"Mm. Yes. That's me."

"I'm Special Agent Hector Santos with the Philadelphia district field office."

Sam's brain snapped to attention. He stood to stretch, switching the phone to his other ear.

"The agent working on the Allentown case?" Sam asked.

"Yes, that's me."

"Thank you for returning my call," Sam said. "I know how busy you are right now."

"As your message relayed, you know I also worked on the case you're following—Jenna Turner," Hector said. "You wanted to know if I could pass along any information that might help with your investigation."

"Yes, that's right," Sam said. He was amazed. He knew he could probably get some information from the FBI office, but he figured it would only be through his Allentown police force connections. It wasn't often the FBI worked directly with a private investigator.

"As you know, we tend to partner with the police force on cases like this. They share with you what they think you need to help with your old case files."

"Yes, I know that and appreciate the fact you've called me."

"I'm not prepared to give you details on the current case in Allentown, Mr. Osborne.

Allentown P.A. will help you with that. I wanted you to know one relative thing, however, because it's the reason I've been called into this case."

Sam sat back down, fascinated that an agent was sharing information directly.

"I wasn't called in because of the similarities with the current case, Mr. Osborne. I was called in as a follow up to a case several years ago; several months before Jenna Turner's disappearance. We had another kidnapping from the same mall as this current case. The boy was never found."

After spending the remaining few hours of the early morning in his bed, Sam got up, and walked to his kitchen, grabbed a quick breakfast, and went downstairs to his office. It was Saturday. Casey was home with her family. He called and asked her to look into the case from three years ago the FBI agent had mentioned.

Sam then read over all his notes and called Captain McCoy. Though it was the weekend, he knew Bob would be in his office; the captain was working third shift and off hours for a few weeks to assess the condition of the night crews. The police captain would be getting ready to head home about now.

"Bob," Sam said. "I'm on my way to Ohio tomorrow—the western side of the state. I need a favor."

Yawning, Bob asked in a tired voice, "What do you need?"

"Can you get in touch with the police force for St. Mary's—Auglaize County, Ohio, and tell them who I am and what I'm investigating. You know small town cops don't particularly care to be doing personal favors for someone they don't know, but I could use some help. Ask them whether the names John and Natalie Collins or Nancy Maddox are familiar to them. If you get a good feel for whoever you're talking to, maybe you can ask if they'd check the town's real estate office and see about a John Becker who owns property in the area."

Bob seemed to wake up then, interest evident in his voice. "What's this all about? You found something out?"

"Yes, I think so. First, I wanted to pass along that I got a call from the FBI agent in Allentown last night. He was brought into the case because of a similar case there in that town three years ago."

"I don't remember the case. But I wasn't head of police here yet. And what does that have to do with Ohio?"

"Nothing directly. Just passing along that info. I'll have Casey call you later to see what your department can share and report what she learns. She's doing some initial research on the old case. In the meantime, though, I wanted to report what we've learned. I'm pretty sure, Bob, that Natalie Collins and her husband John kidnapped Jenna, and that Natalie is Nancy Maddox, the daughter of Charles Maddox and an old school mate of Maggie's. I'll have Casey send over what we've learned. I'm going to Ohio to check out where the Maddox family moved after Columbia, Maryland then on to St. Mary's to check on a cottage the Collins rented from John Becker. I just need an intro to that police force that comes from you, not me."

Bob chuckled. "You don't ask much from a guy who was just up all night and on his way home. But good work on making the connection between Natalie and Nancy Maddox."

He yawned again.

"It sounds like you've gotten pretty far with this. Let me grab some sleep, then I'll do what I can, and the burgers are on you again this month."

Maggie was ready Sunday morning when Sam pulled the car into her drive. They'd agreed they might as well get started on the drive to Ohio on Sunday, and then spend a night somewhere depending on the timing and what they found.

Sam leaned over and kissed her softly on the cheek, then put her suitcase in the trunk.

"Get any sleep the last few nights?" he asked once they were on their way.

"It wasn't easy," she answered. "I kept running over everything in my mind. I can't believe I didn't recognize Nancy Maddox, as many times as I visited the store. I usually sought out Francine, but Natalie helped a few times."

She was studying her hands, which were folded neatly in her lap.

"I have to admit. I spent as much time thinking about you as I did Jenna."

Sam took his eyes off the road for only a moment to glance in her direction, a question on his face.

Maggie looked up, then over at him, a small smile playing on her lips.

"You aren't so good for my sleep, Sam."

Sam's eyes returned to the road, but he was grinning broadly.

Maggie continued.

"You make me feel young and foolish. I'm forty-two, but I think I have my first crush."

They laughed in unison.

"That makes two of us."

He said nothing more, though, and neither did Maggie. They rode in companionable silence, glad they'd admitted their foolishness, but knowing now was not the time to explore the feelings.

Sam had only an address for where the Maddox family had lived in Youngstown. He didn't really expect to find anything while they were there. But Youngstown was on the way to St. Mary's, and he'd learned in his many years of investigation that telephone calls and the Internet did not suffice when it came to digging deeper than the police could go.

Sam parked at the curb across from the Maddox home and began with that house. The residents that lived there now hadn't even heard of the Maddox family. They'd purchased the home from another couple whose name they didn't recall and had no idea how long the other couple had owned the house.

Sam stood on the curb next to his car, surveying his surroundings to get a feel for the area. He knew the Maddox family had rented the home, but they'd stayed there for nearly five years. Surely someone would remember them.

The neighborhood was one of those built in the 1950s or 1960s, all the homes constructed of the same brown brick, and distinguishable only by placement of windows or inclusion of different features the builder had offered. On this street, those options appeared to be a carport, white columns at the front entrance, and a choice of shutter styles.

For the most part, the homes and yards were neatly kept with the occasional bike left outside by children. The residents who lived here now were probably second or third-generation purchasers who liked the retro look, the reasonable price, and the look of real brick, Sam assumed.

One home kitty corner from the Maddox address stood out for him though. The shutters were worn and slightly shabby—the home was in need of some minor repairs. Unlike some of the other homes, the house looked like it hadn't been power-washed or repainted in many years. The yard was neat, but sparse in shrubbery. The trees in the yard, however, looked bigger than other yards, some of which had no trees at all. Sam motioned for Maggie to follow him then headed for that house.

It took almost five minutes for someone to answer the door, and Sam was not at all surprised to see an elderly, slow-moving woman.

"I'm sorry to disturb you, miss, but I'm detective Sam Osborne. This is my friend Maggie Turner. We're seeking some information about a former neighbor of yours," Sam said.

The woman giggled, startling both Maggie and Sam.

"I haven't been a 'miss' in 60 or 70 years,

young man. And to tell you the truth, I don't know many of my neighbors anymore, except the Wilsons next door of course. Such a nice couple. Always mowing my lawn and offering to trim my tree, and such darling kids."

"Actually, the people we are seeking information on would have lived here almost twenty years ago," Sam interrupted.

"Well, in that case," the woman said, swinging open the door. "If anyone would remember them, it would be me. Won't you come in? I just brewed a pot of coffee."

Maggie and Sam followed the woman into the interior, which, like the outside of the house, was neat, but worn. The old woman motioned to an overstuffed sofa, then walked into an adjoining kitchen. Sam took the time she was gone to look around, his natural curiosity piqued. Maggie sat and also studied her environment.

The woman's living room was covered with pictures of people—every surface, every wall had framed photographs that drew both Sam's and Maggie's eyes. Sam picked up one of the largest, which was an eight-by-ten that rested on the coffee table.

"That's my whole clan," the woman said, returning with a tray, cream and sugar, and three steaming mugs. She set her load down before taking the frame out of Sam's hands.

"There's my dear Robert, of course," she said, pointing at a man, a dreamy look on her face. "He passed almost seventeen years ago now. And there's Tommy, Susy, Marigold, and our youngest, Stan. He actually lives the closest now… that's me on the right. Oh, I'm sorry. Let me introduce myself. I'm Betty Grande."

Betty sat on a nearby armchair, reaching forward to put the picture back on the table, then choosing one of the mugs from the tray.

Sam had noticed the house in the picture—the same one they were sitting in now. He wondered briefly how all those kids fit into a home so small.

"I guess you've lived in this area a long time?"

"Robert and I bought this place more than 50 years ago. We kept saying it was time to move, but we loved the neighborhood, our kids all had lots of friends… and well, Robert and I never had much money."

"Then maybe you remember this family I'm here about. The name was Maddox, and it would have been a mother and her two children, Nancy and Chuck. The father, Charles Senior may have been joined at some point also. He would have gotten out of prison in about 1992."

Betty looked shocked.

"Charles Maddox was in prison? I didn't

know that, and I'm pretty sure none of the neighbors did either or that would have been a juicy piece of gossip. I remember the family, yes. And I remember Charles coming home, but I thought he was in the military."

"Did you know them well?" Maggie asked.

"No, not really. As I recall, the mom... oh, what was her name. Gretta?"

"Gladys?" Sam prodded.

Betty nodded as the memory fell into place.

"Gladys. Of course. Gladys was rather stand-offish. I guess I understand why now. I had no idea she was hiding something!"

"But you remember them, Betty?" Maggie prodded.

Betty was nodding her head.

"The kids were mostly grown when they moved here. The boy was still in school; the girl was out by then. My middle girl, Marigold, was about her age. They had both just graduated from high school and worked together at the Burger King down the lane. Then the girl... what was her name..." Betty tapped her own forehead, trying to remember. "Nancy. That was it. Nancy Maddox. She moved somewhere, but she and Marigold kept in contact for a short while... at least until the Maddox girl just sort of dropped off the face of the earth."

"She disappeared?" Sam asked.

"She moved to some place in Ohio, but came back quite a bit. She and Marigold kept in touch, long enough that Nancy had Marigold in her wedding. I remember we spent a fortune on a dress. But as far as I know, Marigold never heard from Nancy again after that wedding. I guess this John fellow whisked her off to some place new…"

"You mean John Collins," Maggie interjected.

"No. No. That doesn't sound quite right."

"It was another name?" Sam asked.

"It wasn't Collins, no. Now what was his name?" She tapped one bent finger against her forehead. "What was that name…Oh, excuse me a second." Betty lifted herself slowly out of the chair and left the room.

Sam looked at Maggie. She looked back at him. They shrugged their shoulders at the same time.

When Betty returned, she carried a scrap-book, which she'd already opened. She set it down and pointed to something, which Sam and Maggie saw was an old wedding invitation.

"She married John Becker on July 2, 1995."

Back in the car a half hour later, Maggie tore through her bag until she located what she was looking for and handed it to Sam.

"The papers for the rental in St. Mary's say that John and Natalie Collins rented the cottage from John Becker," Maggie said.

"Yes, I know," Sam said. "I think we're onto something, Maggie."

CHAPTER TWENTY-FIVE

WHEN THEY LEFT THE Ohio turnpike and were almost to Lima, Ohio, Sam called Bob to check in with him. Maggie had taken over the driving.

Bob had had luck with the local police force in the St. Mary's area and with the real estate office.

"The police there are expecting you, though they weren't too happy that I wouldn't give more information. The police chief in St. Mary's, however, was a coffee pal with the local realtor and made a call on your behalf. There is a John Becker who is an absent landlord in the area. He owns a cottage. Becker apparently calls the real estate office every so often and asks the realtor to make sure the cottage is cleaned for a rental. She said, however, that the last time was over two years ago."

Bingo, Sam thought. But he didn't say anything. He'd get the local police force involved and thank his friend later. But Bob wasn't finished.

"According to the realtor, the cottage is very isolated. It sits in a grove of trees a short distance from St. Mary's lake. If it had been closer to that lake, it would have had to be placed on the public sewer system. It's just far enough away to have its own septic tank."

"Sam, are you thinking this was some kind of hideaway for the kidnappers?" Bob asked.

"All I know is that John Becker is connected to John and Natalie Collins. I'm going to check it out, then I'll call and update you," Sam said. "Casey will be calling you probably today and updating you on what she digs up on the old Allentown case."

Bob then gave Sam the name of the real estate agent and hung up. Sam called Casey.

"Yes, Sam, the case three years ago in Allentown was also a snatching from a store. The parents in that case fully cooperated with the cops. A ransom demand was made, but the money was never picked up, like with the current case in Allentown. No mysterious bag, however, and in the case three years ago, a neighbor was a main suspect for a while. They could never connect him directly. Do you think all three cases are connected somehow?"

Although Casey had posed the question, she knew Sam well enough to know she wasn't getting speculation as an answer. She got practicality.

"Can you put together a few facts you've learned and contact Bob McCoy, Casey? I'm sure the FBI and the police will do their own follow up, but you may as well give Bob some preliminaries."

By the time Sam and Maggie arrived in Lima, it was after six, and they were both famished. They stopped at a Holiday Inn only to find out the local homecoming was the next night. Even though the accommodating clerk called around, she had the only room left in the immediate area: a single room with two beds. Maggie and Sam grabbed it, and then went in search of a restaurant.

When Sam saw Giovanni's, he decided to spring for a nice meal. Italian food was one of his greatest passions, and the place looked clean and lively with many cars parked around the lot.

He wasn't disappointed. As the two sat sipping glasses of dry, slightly fruity red wine and letting the hours in the car seep slowly out of their joints, he sighed in satisfaction. The salads and rolls had been excellent, and Sam knew from experience that was probably a good sign the meal to come would be, too. They hadn't said much, but felt in tune, knowing they were working together on a common goal.

Sam looked over at Maggie, who was busy studying the people around her. He cleared his throat, bringing her eyes around to his face.

"Tell me about Jenna," was all Sam said. He hadn't asked her much about her child beyond the facts he needed to start the case. He knew what talking about a missing child could do to the parent whose heart was breaking, and he didn't want to feel the pain. However, they were now headed together down a road that could very well end in tragedy, and he suddenly wanted to share her anguish.

Maggie didn't even ask Sam what he wanted to know. She reached for Sam's hand.

"She has a heart that somehow seems way too big for a… well, she'd be six years old now."

Maggie settled back against the booth, and her eyes reflected the fact that her mind had left the room for a journey to the past. "Earlier in the year Jenna was taken, a very good friend of mine died suddenly. It was an older woman I met because she needed help selling off her family home so that she could move to a place that would accommodate her age. It took almost a year to get someone interested in the home, and during that time, I got to know the woman pretty well. She refused to move in with one of her kids, who all wanted her. Instead, she'd picked out a retirement place in the Washington, D.C. area that catered to active seniors.

"While it was that independent spirit that made me admire her, it was how she felt about her own home that pushed me over the edge and made me fall in love with her. She wouldn't sell to just anyone. She wanted a young couple about to start a family, and she waited until she found just the right one."

Maggie's eyes returned to the table and Sam's face.

"Anyway, the woman died from a heart attack just before she was about to move into her new home. Chad could not understand why it upset me so—after all, she was just 'a client', an old lady who had already lived a full life. But my little girl saw her mom crying and crawled into bed with me. She put her tiny arms around me and didn't ask questions or act scared. She just knew I needed her help."

Sam was glad that the meal was almost over. Despite the crowded restaurant, tears were falling onto Maggie's plate. She made no sound; she gave no apologies for crying in the middle of a crowd. He bent over and took her hand in both of his, rubbing the back of it gently with one of his. Maggie continued.

"She was like that from a very young age: empathetic beyond her years. I had a pretty bad marriage that I managed to ignore for my four plus years with Jenna. Maybe she sensed the pain of the relationship. Maybe she was just born with that calm understanding. I don't know. I only know our days together were filled with the excitement of childhood, and I loved every minute of it."

Sam put his arm around Maggie and drew her body to his. She turned her head into the solid muscles of his shoulder.

"Can I interest you in some dessert?" the waiter asked. "The pastry chef made some fresh cannoli this morning."

"Just the check." Sam's voice was slightly raspy.

Back in the hotel, Maggie suddenly looked uncomfortable as she laid her suitcase on one of the beds and sat next to the suitcase, and then looked over at the other bed.

Sam just grinned and sat down across from her on the second bed.

"I'm sorry about the one room. But we are two older adults who are tired from a long car trip, glasses of wine, and emotion, and I think you trust me enough to know I'm not going to ravish you."

That made Maggie chuckle, open her suitcase, and got out a nightgown and robe. She headed for the bathroom and its soothing shower. At the door, she turned back to Sam.

"And who says I don't want you to ravish me, dear Sam? It's been an awfully long time."

Maggie didn't see Sam's eyes widen slightly. She shut the door and tore off the day's wrinkled clothes, then stepped into the shower, letting the hot water coax away the ache in her muscles and her heart.

Sam flopped back on the bed, his eyes glued to the ceiling, his body feeling a different kind of ache. He knew how bad an idea it was to get involved with a client, but it didn't help the hunger. He was pretty sure now that Maggie felt the same longing. Neither, however, had had time to fully explore how they felt about each other.

When he heard the hair dryer start up, he made himself get up and get his bag off the floor. Thank goodness he always packed a set of gym shorts in case he felt like working out or going for a run. He sat on the bed holding the shorts and a t-shirt, waiting for his turn for the shower.

After a few minutes, however, he rose and went to the bathroom door, opening it quietly and catching Maggie's startled eyes in the mirror. Her sand-colored curls were fanned out in every direction, her hair still slightly damp.

Sam walked up behind her, and put one hand on hers, taking the dryer from her and finishing the job, then setting the dryer down and picking up her hairbrush. He began to gently brush her hair, not meeting her eyes in the mirror, just busying himself with the task.

Maggie leaned against his solid body and closed her eyes, letting his strength seep into her bones. She didn't know when he laid down the brush, but she felt his breath on her neck as he lifted her hair and began nibbling on her neck. The nibbles turned into soft kisses.

The next sensation she felt was his hands on her belly, slowly caressing her skin through the nightgown, then finding their way to her breasts. His breathing was labored, and he began to groan softly. Maggie didn't want to open her eyes, didn't want to think. She just wanted to feel.

Sam's hands moved southward and his nibbling at her neck and shoulder resumed. He caressed her hips, then her thighs, and when his hands found the hem of her nightgown, then made contact with her skin, Maggie could no longer contain her own moans of pleasure. She opened her eyes, turned to his hard body and crushed herself against him, grabbing handfuls of hair and seeking his lips with her own. Despite the passion and deepness of the kiss, Sam managed to scoop her up and carry her towards the bed.

He made no comment as he gently laid her down, her nightgown discarded on the way. He let his eyes travel the length of her curves, and when they found her violet eyes, he saw that they were a shade darker and full of passion.

At 8:30 a.m. the alarm on Sam's watch went off. Maggie's hand grabbed the covers to throw them off. Sam reached over and pulled them back, then snuggled up closer to Maggie's skin. She felt his erection against her backside and laughed.

"Aren't we a little old for this?" she whispered, her words lost in the pillow as Sam nibbled at her ear.

"No. Such. Thing." His hoarse voice replied. But he stopped, sighed, and rose on one elbow, his head resting on his hand, his eyes seeking her eyes.

"Something tells me I could do this with you when we're a hundred and one," he said.

Maggie smiled and reached for him, ready to be swept away again to wonderland, every nerve in her body ready for the trip.

CHAPTER TWENTY-SIX

THE MEETING WITH REALTOR Gail Brown wasn't until eleven, so Sam suggested Maggie go back to sleep. She was wide-awake, however, and offered to get coffee and breakfast from the hotel breakfast room.

When she returned, the two sat together on the bed and munched English muffins and fruit. The silence in the room grew heavy. It wasn't awkward, just filled with two people's deep thoughts.

When they were done with their breakfast and sipping coffee on the bed, Sam looked over and saw Maggie staring at him.

"You feel it, too. Don't you?" she asked. She wasn't talking about what had gone on between the two of them.

Sam's eyes closed and he cradled his Styrofoam cup in his lap.

"It doesn't make any sense, Maggie."

His eyelids fluttered open and his brown eyes sought the intensity of violet staring at him. "Yes," he admitted. "I think we're getting close to finding out what happened somehow, and I feel a sense of urgency I do not understand."

But he got up from the bed, straightened his shoulders and looked at his watch. "First things first. It's almost time to meet with the Brown woman. Do you want to go?"

"I do," she said, rising from the bed and brushing a few errant crumbs from her jeans. "Let's see about this cottage. I feel like if Jenna was ever there, I'd know it."

They drove to St. Mary's and to the office of Gail Brown, a chubby woman in her 60s with white-blue hair and a friendly smile. She affirmed that she handled the rental of John Becker's cottage.

"Chief Higgins said you'd inquired about the cottage. Are you interested in renting it out, then? It's pretty rustic, but it's quiet and close to a lake. Good place for fishing… or honeymooning," she was looking from Sam to Maggie as she said it.

Maggie colored, and exchanged a look with Sam. They both laughed.

Who cared if it was obvious how they felt?

Sam replied, "As much as that idea appeals to me, Mrs. Brown. I'm actually here on business, investigating a possible kidnapping. The cottage may have been used by the kidnappers. What's your arrangement with Mr. Becker?"

At the word "kidnapping," the real estate agent's eyes had gone round and the smile disappeared.

"No one has rented or inquired about that cottage in several years," she said.

She explained, however, that she'd been responsible for handling any rentals that did come in and had also inherited the task of periodically checking up on the property. She had done so about six months ago.

Gail said she'd met with Becker a few times early in the agreement to set up the deal, but had only talked with him by phone since then. She vaguely remembered him as a large man who was good-looking, but couldn't remember much else about his appearance.

"Can we see inside the cottage?" Sam asked.

Gail pushed her chair back from the desk as if she were about to rise. She clutched her throat with one plump hand.

"I have a key, of course. But don't you need a search warrant or something?"

Sam let a few moments pass before answering.

He sought out Gail's eyes, and even though he and Maggie were driven only by instinct, decided to be honest about the situation and their feeling that time was important.

"As you know, we've talked with Chief Higgins and I'm sure I can get local authorities involved in all this… eventually. A warrant, however, will require time we don't feel we have. All we're really asking is to see the inside of a rural cottage that you've said hasn't been used in a long time. Call the Lancaster police department if you doubt who we are and speak with Captain Bob McCoy. He'll vouch for us."

Sam knew Bob wouldn't be in until that night, but his gamble paid off.

The agent pulled her chair back to the desk and took a deep breath.

"Well, I suppose if this is important, it won't hurt," she said with a shaky voice. "I'll take you out now."

She reached for a key lying on top of paperwork on her desk. The fact it was there affirmed she had already been prepared to "show" the cottage. Sam wondered why she'd hesitated, and then decided she wasn't used to the drama of a crime and just didn't know how to handle it.

The cottage was set far enough away from the road that most people would pass right by its driveway without glancing towards the structure. The setting was beautiful, with long overflowing branches of trees shading the roof, vines climbing up the walls, and the lake twinkling in the background. The house's exterior, however, looked like it had succumbed to weathering and time. It reminded Sam of the house in his dream about Davie, though it wasn't quite as ramshackle and the property sported no barn.

Before climbing the rickety porch stairs to get inside, Maggie and Sam walked the yard, finding nothing significant until they came to a gravestone.

"Kate Morgan Becker, b. February 4, 1974; d. February 6, 1993." Beside the grave marker was a small, crude cross that was made from branches of a tree.

The site, while peaceful, made Maggie shudder.

"Why is this woman buried out here so far from everything?" she said.

"And how is she related to John Becker?" Sam added.

When they made their way back to the front of the house, the real estate agent was standing on the porch by the door.

"I know it doesn't look like much from the outside, but I think you'll find the inside much different." She unlocked the door and swung it gently open.

Maggie stepped in first.

"Oh my. It's actually quite lovely."

The furnishings inside were no newer than the outside, but it was obvious someone had once cared. Much of the furniture looked like it had been made from trees in the neighboring woodlands, and while nothing looked expensive, it all seemed to match. Red-checked curtains in the kitchen window matched a red tablecloth on a kitchen table. The few pieces of furniture that weren't wood were covered with gold slipcovers that had to have been hand-sewn because they fit so well. A large stone fireplace was the center of the living area.

Maggie and Sam began a thorough search of the place, rousing up dust as they went.

Gail Brown, who stood by and watched, sighed deeply. "Oh, it needs a thorough cleaning, I know. But I've always found this place really charming. Mr. Becker must have had a real knack for finding and fixing up things."

"It's like an enchanted cottage in a fairytale," Maggie exclaimed. She was standing with her hands on her hips, a smudge of dirt on her nose.

Sam nodded his head, looking around. He knew he had very little taste as far as furnishings, but the cottage and its giant stone fireplace made him want to settle into a comfortable chair and reach for a good book.

As if she'd heard his thoughts, Maggie sat down on one of the welcoming rocking chairs and let out a large, slow sigh.

"I wonder if the original creator of this place was the woman on the gravestone."

She looked at Gail.

"Did you ever meet Kate Morgan Becker?" she asked.

Gail tilted her head trying to remember.

"Yes, yes, I believe I met a young woman here once a long time ago. She had to be Kate Becker. As I recall, she was a tiny thing, a petite woman and pretty young," Gail Brown said, smiling. "I think that she was John's wife, or at least they were companions, not siblings. I don't know why that sticks in my head, though. I do remember that their solitude caused some talk among townsfolk." Suddenly she peered more closely at Maggie.

"Say, she wasn't a relative of yours, was she?"

Maggie looked baffled.

"Why would you say that? No, I've never met the woman. I've never been here before."

Gail nodded her head. "Of course. But the eyes. Those violet eyes of yours. I've never seen eyes that color. I just remember how startling the color was on the young woman."

Sam and Maggie exchanged a puzzled look. Sam turned back to Gail.

"Do you remember anything else about her, Mrs. Brown? When did you meet her?"

"Oh, I was here just a few moments. I only got a glimpse of her. She wasn't very friendly, though she was certainly polite. I drove all the way here to give her a package, and she didn't invite me in."

"A package?" Sam prodded.

Gail then looked embarrassed.

"As it turned out, it wasn't for her. The name was Jack Stone, who lived across the lake. Wrong address. So I guess I couldn't really blame her."

Seeing the wrinkled brows of both Sam and Maggie, Gail continued.

"John Becker was known by only a few people in town; the Beckers kept to themselves. I don't think many people besides me ever caught a glimpse of the elusive Kate Becker. People wondered if the two were hiding something or someone out here. John must have done all the shopping because people saw him come into town. The few times he stopped in the office, he was alone. Once he moved away, I never saw him again."

"Do you remember a funeral or a death notice or anything about when she died?" Maggie asked.

Gail shook her head. "No. I guess that was too far back. I really don't remember anything. There might be something about her death in the newspaper, though. Maybe they ran some kind of notice or obituary or something?" Gail suggested.

"I was just wondering about that," Sam agreed, looking at his watch. "It's fairly early. I'm sure I can still catch the newspaper office open. Want to go look?" he asked.

Maggie sighed, tiredness evident in her voice.

"Not really. I'd rather just stay and try to get a sense of whether Jenna was here. I know it's a lot to ask, Ms. Brown, but do you think I could stay a bit?

Gail looked unsure. As they were combing through the house they had explained to Gail that it was Maggie's daughter who had been kidnapped. Gail said she'd never seen a child or signs of a child at the cottage, but promised to check her records at the time of the kidnapping to see if John and Natalie Collins had been at the cottage. She glanced at her watch.

Maggie's eyes sought out Gail's.

"I know you need to get back to the office and I assure you, I'll take good care of this cottage, but I'd really like some more time. Could I stay here just a little while? Sam and I will be glad to check in with you after he picks me up. Please, I want to see if there are any signs of my little girl."

Gail looked from Maggie to Sam, then around the cottage. Her face softened.

"I supposed there is no one I could tattle to, actually. I haven't heard from John Becker in many months, and it's evident from the dust no one has been here in quite a while. If you think it will help with your hunt for your child, stay for a bit. I do need to get back to my office, and I can show Sam where the newspaper office is."

Sam bent over and kissed Maggie on her forehead. Then he swiped at the smudge of dirt on her face.

"Okay. You rest," he said. "I'll pick you up in an hour or so."

After they left, Maggie wandered through the cottage again, picking up objects and putting them back down. Taking a kitchen towel from a drawer, she began dusting off objects as she searched. *Who was this young couple that had made the cottage their home? And how was this place connected to Natalie and her husband?*

When Maggie came to the bedroom, she laid back on the wrought iron bed, which was devoid of bedclothes, but covered by a clean-looking mattress. She closed her eyes. After what seemed like only a few minutes, her eyes flew open and she sat up.

Had she really fallen asleep? Had it been a dream? She had seen Jenna sitting on the edge of this bed. A large man had been slowly combing Jenna's blond locks, gently pushing and pulling the brush through her thick hair.

Maggie swung her legs over the side of the bed and rubbed her face. *Was she going nuts?* She stretched, and then felt something flutter against her calf and reached down to pull out a piece of pink ribbon caught between the mattress and bed frame. Suddenly, Maggie's hands were shaking and tears began falling.

That's how Sam found her a few minutes later, still on the bed, still holding the ribbon and crying.

"What's wrong?" Sam asked, fear reflected in his eyes. He encircled the wrist of the hand holding the ribbon and took it from her. "What is this?"

"It's Jenna's hair ribbon," Maggie said. "She was here."

"It's just a scrap of cloth. How can you know that?" Sam asked.

Maggie snatched the ribbon back and turned it over. On the underside, written in magic marker, was JLT.

"Jennifer Lyn Turner! She had this identity

thing going, Sam. The minute she was old enough to discern letters, I taught her what her initials looked like. JLT were the first three letters she learned. The day she finally understood what the letters meant, she insisted we mark all her clothes, even her socks. I humored her for a little while that day, and even got so far as to label her hair ribbons!"

Tears were streaming down Maggie's face as she held the ribbon close to her cheek.

Sam took Maggie into his arms, but said nothing. Once her tears were spent, he got up from the bed, his mood now decisive.

"It's probably time to get back to the hotel, but let's give it one more go-over before we leave. There has to be something we're missing."

The two began an even-more-thorough search of the cottage and its small loft, pulling out every drawer and looking at their undersides, taking the mattress off the bed and looking underneath. As they went, Maggie queried Sam about what he had learned in town.

"I went back to the weeks after she died, but there was no funeral notice. If she's buried out there in this yard, it's likely that John Becker dug the grave himself. It's odd, but not unheard of. I have to wonder, though, why John didn't report her death, if she was his wife."

He was running his fingers along the tops of

the cabinets. Neither he nor Maggie had found anything that shed further light on who had lived or stayed in the cottage.

After another thirty minutes, Sam sat down on a living room chair to rest.

His eyes wandered the room, and then alighted on the floor. He turned toward Maggie.

"Did you see anything like a screwdriver when you were searching the kitchen?"

"I think so," Maggie said as she rose and walked into the kitchen. She withdrew a small screwdriver from a drawer and took it to Sam, who was bent on the floor at a heat register. With screwdriver in hand, he worked on the old screws.

"What is it? What are you doing?"

"It's a long shot. But when I was a kid, this was a favorite hiding place for my boyhood treasures. I ruined a few baseball cards because the heat melted their waxy coating, but most things came out fine. In this house, however, with that giant fire place, I doubt they even had to turn the heat on very often, and if they were pressed for money, they probably couldn't afford the central heat."

The register cover was off, and Sam was running his hand down the sides of the vent. Maggie saw the second his hand hit pay dirt.

"Whoa," he exclaimed. "What is this?"

He had extended his arm as far as he could and was now drawing out a leather Bible. Blowing off a layer of dust, he began flipping pages.

"What is it?" Maggie asked.

"Looks like it's a family Bible of some kind. I'm not sure why it was hidden away…"

As his fingers reached the end of the book, he suddenly looked up at Maggie, excitement on his face.

"There's someone's recording of events here at the end where the blank pages usually are. I can't make out what it says too well—we're losing our light and I left the flashlight in my car. But it's not that old. It starts out, 'It is the year 1993 and I am…' " he looked up at Maggie again. " 'I am Johann Becker…' "

Sam got up off the ground and dusted his clothes.

"Let's take it back to the motel. After we've had something to eat, we can read it together," Sam said. He shut the book.

"Oh, I don't know if I can wait!" Maggie said.

Sam put his arm around her and was already leading her out.

"Maggie, honey. It's not likely to be connected to Jenna in any way with a date so long ago. But maybe it can shed some light on her abductors and how they are connected to this cottage and John Becker."

CHAPTER TWENTY-SEVEN

AFTER PICKING UP SUB sandwiches and sodas, Sam and Maggie were back in the room, sitting side by side on the motel bed, the Bible between them.

"Ready?" Sam asked Maggie.

"Ready," she replied as he opened the Bible and flipped to the end. Maggie took it from him and read.

I am Johann Becker and I have murdered Gerald Morgan. You would think that I would have some regrets, but I do not. I write this note not to confess my supposed sins, but as proof to myself that I have no regrets. And to put down on paper how much I loved my Kate.

Maggie gasped and clutched her throat, but continued to read.

I have no regrets because if I had killed the bastard sooner, Kate would be alive and I would have a son or daughter.

The next few words on the page were blurred as if the paper had gotten wet, but Maggie was able to pick out enough words to figure out what he was saying.

I will never regret my short time with my beloved, no matter what happens with the rest of my life. Kate saved me at a time when no one in the whole world cared if I lived or died. Certainly not the family I grew up in. I don't think those Bible-thumping morons ever looked for me after I left them.

I want the world to know who Kate was and how we came to be together. When I was seven, my family moved from Cincinnati, Ohio where we had a nice house in a good neighborhood to a farm in northern Ohio. My stupid father thought all things that had to do with the city had suddenly become "evil."

He took my mom, my brother and me to the middle of Amish country, and plunked us down on a farm. Eventually, my parents fell under the spell of the "simple people" who were our neighbors. After kowtowing to those neighbors for a year, they eventually let us into their precious church.

While my younger brother Eli had no

problem with this backwards lifestyle, I hated it from the start. I wanted my television back, my cool clothes, the family car, fast food, and my Walkman and Nintendo. I spent most of my growing up time in trouble both at school and at home. I kept out of jail but just barely.

There was only one thing the Amish did that made sense to me and that was rumspringa. That's when your Amish parents are told to be tolerant of your behavior and let you go out and experience what they call the "English" ways of life. You're supposed to eventually choose the Amish church. Learn. Unfortunately, my rumspringa resulted in me getting a friend pregnant. She was my one true friend at the time, Rebecca, and I'm sorry for what I did to her. She put up with a lot of drunkenness, and she let me ramble on about how unhappy I was. She hid me from my parents several times so I could sober up. Unfortunately, she also liked me a lot, and eventually gave in to my attempts to seduce her.

I just could not do what the Amish community expected and marry her. I knew I would die if I had to live among those people. So I ran. I knew the church would shun me. I simply did not care. I had too much of my life yet to live.

For most of the next year, I wandered from one city in Ohio to another, begging in places big enough for an audience and stealing what I could to stay alive. One day I was almost beaten to death by a group of boys whose drug money I tried to get. I was lying in an alley unable to move when Kate found me. I don't know why, but she got me to safety, then took care of me and nursed me back to life.

Maggie lifted her head for a moment to breathe and let the words sink in.

"I guess we now know who Kate was and what she meant to John Becker, who I have to assume is Johann," she said. She bent her head to continue reading.

Kate was only 16 when I met her, but she already knew a lot about surviving on the streets. I didn't find out why until I'd known her awhile. We started traveling together from city to city helping each other out. After a few weeks of this, she told me how she had come to be a runaway.

She was running from Gerald Morgan, who was her uncle. When she was nine, Gerald came to live with his sister, Kate's mom. Kate said he was handsome and funny and everyone loved his stories. What no one knew was that he started getting into her bed at night when she was nine. She didn't know exactly what was happening at first, but when she did and when she told her no-good mom, the woman did not believe her. Kate never got up the courage to tell her teachers or anyone who might have been able to do something because she truly believed Gerald would kill her.

He was obsessed. As she got older, he talked about marrying her and keeping her protected from all other men. She ran away several times, only to be returned by authorities because she was under age. She got smarter with each escape and by the time I met her, she knew from experience that her greatest challenge to being free was keeping far away from police and other people.

My greatest desire became finding a place where Kate would feel truly safe. This cottage belongs to my family, who abandoned it when they abandoned their life in Cincinnati. I knew it hadn't been used since well before we moved to Amish country. Kate and I made our way here by stealing a car and some people's wallets then hopping a train and walking. We found this house practically uninhabitable, but Kate was not one to give up. With a lot of hard work and many missteps, we figured out how to patch the roof and fix up the place. It became our home. I kept us in food by hunting and the occasional odd job in town.

Eventually, the fear that lived deep within Kate disappeared, and we were really happy. That's what I want people to know about Kate. She was kind and good, and she was happy, if only for a little while.

We spoke our wedding vows by the lake outside this cottage on a beautiful evening with the stars and the nighttime critters as our witnesses.

We were young, naïve, and filled with hope. We were overjoyed when Kate got pregnant.

I don't know how Gerald tracked us down, but he was a policeman, so he had a lot of help. He knew my name through Kate's mom because Kate called her mother to let her know she was okay. I heard such pride in her voice as she told her mom she was now a married lady with a good man looking after her. Gerald must have traced me that way because I used my father's identity. My father didn't give me much in life, but I got his looks and I stole an old driver's license when I ran that helped me out a lot along the way. I convinced the realtor I was the one who owned this cottage by using that identity and it got us this home that brought us so many months of happiness. But it probably also was our weak link.

Maggie lifted her head, tears evident in her eyes. She handed the book to Sam to continue reading, knowing in her heart what was coming.

Sam cleared his throat and began.

Yesterday, Gerald arrived here when I was out doing chores. I heard Kate's screams as he was beating her, and though I ran as fast as I could, I was too late.

I don't know if he intended to kill my Kate, but I know in my heart that she fought him with every inch of her being, anxious to protect our unborn child, as well as me.

Gerald hit her in the head with an iron skillet, and she lay sprawled on the floor when I found her; her eyes were empty and staring at the ceiling. There was blood all over the floor. So much blood.

The bastard stood there looking confused as hell as if he couldn't understand how it had happened. I don't even remember the next few minutes. I know I couldn't have stopped hitting the man if I'd wanted to. At one point, I saw he was an unconscious heap of flesh on the floor, but I didn't care. I got my gun and shot him over and over. Then I dragged that piece of trash to the dump and put it in one of those cars I knew would be crumpled in the morning.

Sam paused to catch his breath, but he was nearly to the end of the notations.

I buried Kate under the yellow apple tree she loved so much. I think she would have liked that. I don't know where I'll go from here, nor do I really care. This life ended yesterday when she died. I am leaving this cottage and running away again. I will find a way to never live on the streets. I will find a way not to be poor. And I hope to kill a few more Gerald Morgans in my life. Killing

can feel good when it's done for the right reasons.
Killing Gerald was for the right reason.
     John Becker
     February 9, 1993.

CHAPTER TWENTY-EIGHT

THE NEXT DAY WAS spent notifying authorities about what they'd found at the cottage and at the back of the Bible as well as the connections they'd made between John/Johann Becker and the Collins. They took a return trip out to the cottage with police and a local FBI agent from Lima, who chastised them for disturbing what was likely a crime scene. After many hours of going over details, Sam put his arm around Maggie and led her back to the car and they drove back to their room.

"At least we know Jenna was here in this town at some point. We'll find them," he whispered to her, as he tucked her into the hotel bed.

Sam sat at the hotel room's desk feeling powerless and numb. He picked up his cell phone.

"Good evening, Casey. I'm sorry to call you at home at night, but I need a favor from Danny."

"Oh, you know he'd do anything. He's in with the baby, cooing and acting like an idiot. You know, the usual after-dinner activity."

Sam chuckled, feeling better just hearing about his happy family back home.

"I'll get him, Sam, but what's up?"

"I need his help, Casey. I know it's after hours, but I have a huge favor to ask that may take some calling around. I'd ask you to do it, but it might come better from a police officer."

"I understand. Let me get him on the phone."

After a brief pause, Danny's low, booming voice came on the line. If he hadn't encouraged the young man in his pursuit of law, Sam would have suggested he be a DJ. As it was, Danny's voice commanded attention, and Sam believed that fact helped the young man in his job.

"Good evening, Sir Plays-a-Lot," Sam kidded. "Think you can handle an extracurricular job?"

Danny laughed. "Anything, you know that. Well anything legal that is."

Sam rubbed his face with his hand and began.

"Do you remember that Amish fellow we helped? The one looking for his runaway nephew?"

"Of course. Wasn't his name Snyder?"

"Nathaniel Snyder, yeah. Do you remember that he gave us a neighbor's number and said we could contact him if we ever needed help with the Amish people or understanding the culture?"

"Sure. He seemed sincere. He was certainly grateful for our help."

"I need you to call in that favor, Danny. He's from an Amish community outside Millersburg, Ohio. I'm staying near St. Mary's. They're a little distance apart, but the Amish keep better track of each other than the non-Amish community. See if we can get him to ask around among neighbors and family whether anyone is familiar with a Becker family here in Ohio. I'm looking for a John or Johann Becker in particular, though I know that's a common name. We may be able to trace them faster through the Amish channels than trying to track them down through public records."

"No problem. I'll call your cell if I learn anything."

Next, Sam called Bob, who reported that the FBI had already contacted him for background details on Sam, Maggie, and the case. Then Sam crawled into bed with Maggie, who lay on her side, her cell phone on the pillow next to her. Although the ribbon had been turned over as evidence, she'd snapped a picture to remind her that she'd been standing where her daughter had stood.

Sam snuggled up to Maggie, spooning her with his body, trying to give her comfort, knowing he could only offer his warmth.

Just before he fell asleep, he envisioned sitting in Lucinda Lovejoy's home, sipping tea. He heard again the psychic's sad voice.

"I feel her reaching out. This sounds peculiar, but her hands are rough."

Mid-morning the next day, while Sam and Maggie were sipping coffee at a local diner, deciding what step to take next, Sam's cell phone rang. Danny's voice was on the line.

"Nate Snyder says there are several Becker family lines in Ohio and Indiana. He's had a chance to talk to several people this morning because they had a church board meeting scheduled. No one knew a John Becker specifically, but there are several Johann Becker's. I'm tracking down the possibilities by contacting local authorities in the three areas mentioned. I should be able to report in a couple of hours," he continued.

"That's great, Danny. Thanks, and please pass along my appreciation to Nathaniel Snyder."

Noticing Maggie's questioning eyes, Sam reported on what he had asked Danny to look into.

"So we're looking for a John/Johann Becker somewhere here in Ohio or close by, right?"

Sam nodded his head and took another sip of his coffee.

"What about the names Eli and Rebecca? Johann Becker's letter in the Bible mentions his brother Eli and how well he adapted to the Amish life as well as this Rebecca who John/Johann got pregnant. Wouldn't they both be grown up by now?"

Sam was back on the phone with Danny, and one hour later, Danny called back. After a brief conversation, Sam hung up and turned to Maggie.

"Someone in Snyder's community knew of an Eli Becker and his wife Rebecca. They live in Hicksville, Ohio."

Maggie's eyes lit up. The fact those two names from Johann's notes were a couple was too much of a coincidence. There had to be a connection.

"There's more, Maggie."

He took her hand.

"Whoever it was that knew of Eli and Rebecca knew enough to report they have a child. They took in this child because the kid's parents were shunned from the Amish community."

Two hours later, the two were packed and in the car on their way to Hicksville, Ohio. Despite Captain McCoy and Chief Higgins' pleas for the two to sit tight and let authorities take care of the investigation, both Maggie and Sam could not follow their advice. At least they were acting on something by driving the hour to Hicksville. Bob had alerted local authorities that the two were headed that way, and Sam had already called ahead and talked to the local police chief.

Maggie stared silently out at the fields they were passing. Many of those fields lay empty. Other fields contained corn stalks still standing strong and sturdy, waiting for their chance at harvest.

Sam's cell phone rang, and despite his vow never to answer when driving, he couldn't help himself. He didn't talk much, however, just listened to the voice on the other end, occasionally nodding and looking over at the anxious face of Maggie. When he was done, he folded the phone up, put it in the console pocket and pulled off the road. He turned to this woman he now knew he loved, and cleared his throat.

"I'm afraid I have some bad news."

CHAPTER TWENTY-NINE

JOHN COLLINS CLOSED HIS eyes and turned his face to the plane window. In truth, he wasn't even tired. He just didn't feel like talking anymore. He had spent two days arguing with Natalie about this trip and the fight in him had dissipated.

He knew a lot of what she said made sense. They'd run through the money they'd made with the last job. And this time, there should be no killing. His gut, however, was telling him it was a mistake.

He usually trusted those instincts, but anger kept getting in the way – anger at his upbringing, the church, his shunning, Kate's death, Natalie's spending, his own hesitancy.

He couldn't understand why he was even questioning this job. Somehow, it didn't feel safe.

He sighed and opened his eyes to stare out at the wing.

What the hell is wrong with me?

He had a drop-dead, gorgeous wife who shared his taste in clothes, food, lifestyle, and sex. John crossed his arms and leaned back against the headrest, determined to get some sleep. But his mind would not leave the past alone.

Kate had died because he couldn't protect her. They'd lived in poverty; they hadn't even had enough money to put in a phone or run the damn heat. He'd known when he buried her and left the cottage behind that he was burying his past, and part of that past was being without money. He'd never been rich, but he'd always found ways since then to live comfortably. Even though some of those "ways" had been disagreeable, he'd become adept at getting beyond the blood or scheming or treachery to a place where life was easier.

He opened his eyes and looked over at Natalie, who apparently had no demons haunting her. She was snoring gently, her perfect breasts rising and falling in a steady rhythm.

By the time John met Natalie, he'd lived in most of the major urban areas of Ohio and Indiana. He'd even lived for several years on the east coast in New York and Boston, though he found he had no tolerance for cities that large. He'd become a skilled thief, a hired thug, and, on more than one occasion, a means to make someone disappear for the right price. By traveling around, he'd developed the ability to slip out of the grasp of local gang members or the more powerful crime families, leaving behind a reputation for willingness to do the dirty work, but not to become attached or loyal.

Ironically, he'd met Natalie during one of his many down times, when he was living off the money he made on a previous job. She'd been an exotic dancer at one of a handful of clubs in Columbus, Ohio that catered to gentlemen. But John had seen right away that she had ambition that went beyond what her twenty-year-old body could provide. They'd had a wild time together, and Natalie hadn't asked him any questions about where the money came from, even after they went back to her old hometown for the elaborate wedding he'd financed. They'd been inseparable since then with Natalie becoming slowly involved in his business affairs and finding creative new ways to bring in cash.

So unlike Kate. And so very unlike the innocent Rebecca, John thought as he watched her sleep.

Maybe it was going back to that area of the country again that was making him uncomfortable. He sighed deeply.

"Johnny," his wife said softly. "Are you sleeping?"

"No," he said. "I'm, unfortunately, very much awake."

"Are you still worried about getting the child?"

"Yes," he whispered. "I just feel it in my gut that it's not a good idea."

"We have to have money. You know that. It's the safest way—and we'll make that young couple so happy—and us happy as well, with a half a million in our hands."

She reached over and grabbed his wrist.

"They deserve to be happy – and so do we. The kid will grow up surrounded by wealth and luxury. What more could you ask?"

"I'm just not sure how Eli will react. I don't think he could ever track me down, but I hate the thought of crossing him," he said.

"He has no way to know who you are now, Johnny. The plane is almost to Fort Wayne. We can't back out now," she said, trying to inject her common sense into the picture.

"Just let me rest, then. I don't want to think about it anymore," John said. He leaned back, turned his head to the window and closed his eyes again.

The truth was, he felt like shit, and it had little to do with the massive amounts of good bourbon they'd shared the night before to toast a new job. He knew only that he would ten times rather rob a bank or shoot a man than take the kid back, but they were out of money, and Natalie was his partner in more ways than sharing a bed. She had helped him find a steady rhythm to his life.

"I owe you," he said softly to the window. But the words were directed to Natalie. She was no Kate or even a Rebecca, but John knew she was loyal and attached to him. She could have easily robbed him blind and deserted him several times. A woman as true as her didn't deserve to be poor. She had been there herself, and she hated it just as much as he did. He would do what they'd planned, and his life would get back to normal.

CHAPTER THIRTY

SAM SAT IN THE passenger's seat of Hicksville Police Chief Steve Morley's squad car, staring out at the farms passing by. They were on their way to the Beckers' home to question Eli and Rebecca. However, it had turned from a mission to rescue Jenna to an inquiry about the boy the Beckers had taken in, and the county police were on their way as a backup and to take them in for questioning.

Sam turned back to Maggie, feeling powerless. Her tears were gentle and silent, but Sam knew how much she was hurting.

"Maggie," Sam said. "I know how disappointed you are to find out the child at the Beckers is not Jenna – I swear we'll go back over everything and we'll find out what happened to her as well. It's good this boy is alive and well. This is our link to the kidnappers. It's just a step in the process…but it's a giant step."

"I know," Maggie said. She dried her eyes on a Kleenex, but the tears were still falling. "I know you'll do what you can. I know I was stupid to get my hopes up. It's just… just that…"

"You thought we would find her now. I know. But maybe since this kid is still alive, Jenna is alive as well. Maybe John and Natalie are not the hardened criminals we pictured."

Maggie blew her nose gently, swallowed hard and then was quiet. Tears were useless. They were lucky to be allowed to come along for the questioning. This trip would not end in finding Jenna. Maybe it would bring home another child, if Eli Becker's "son" turned out to be someone John and Natalie took. At the least, it might connect authorities with the elusive Johann/ John Becker. That was something… wasn't it?

When they pulled into the Becker's long dirt road, they saw another car parked close to the house.

"That can't be my backup," Police Chief Morley noted. "It takes twenty or thirty minutes to get here from the county seat. It's only been ten since I called them. You two better stay with the car."

All three people got out of the car, and the police chief took a gun he had in the glove department with him. It wasn't likely he'd have to use it with the Amish, but a crime may well have been committed.

The chief stood scratching his head, trying to decide if he needed to wait for backup.

"I just find it difficult to believe that the Beckers would be part of this," he said. "Or any of the Amish for that matter. I'm going to check this out. I'll let you know if it's okay to come in."

He shrugged and approached the home, which was still a hundred feet away. They hadn't wanted to alert anyone that they were there.

Sam and Maggie watched as Chief Morley stepped onto a grey-planked porch and knocked loudly on the door. They saw a tall, thin man dressed in Amish clothes open the door, say a few words, and then attempt to slam the door shut. The captain put his foot out to catch the door, and said a few more words, which caused the Amish man to finally open the door. The captain went inside.

Maggie and Sam stood at the car, feeling anxious and eager to talk to Eli Becker, the brother of the man who had taken Jenna. They understood the captain's need for caution, however, and kept glancing back at the main road, waiting for backup.

Another ten minutes went by with no sign of another police car, and Sam began to get anxious. If everything was under control, why hadn't the captain come back out? Sam glanced at the extra car.

"I'm going up to the house," he announced.

"And I'm going with you," Maggie said. Sam knew he wouldn't be able to change her mind. Even if it wasn't her child inside, she was a mother, and her instinct was to make sure the child was safe.

Instead of knocking on the front door, the two approached as quietly as they could and went to stand beside the window. Sam glanced quickly inside.

"I can't see anyone," he whispered. When he turned back to Maggie, he saw her hand on the knob. The door was unlocked.

Sam wanted to shout out her name and tell her she was moving too fast. Instinct kept him from acting. Something just didn't feel right. Instead, he followed her as she slipped in the front door.

The entryway was as plain and gray as the outside of the house. A few pegs on a rack held heavy-looking woolen outer coats. Three pairs of rubber boots were stacked neatly on the floor beneath the coats.

They stepped cautiously past the rack towards the back of the house where they heard voices, though they couldn't make out the words.

This is a mistake, Sam thought. *Wait for back up.*

Maggie crept forward slowly towards the sound, past doorways on both the left and right. Suddenly, they both heard a voice from one of those doorways.

"I don't really want to shoot you, whoever you are, but turn around slowly."

Maggie pivoted to her right side and froze. Sam's body matched her motion. They'd been passing a sitting room, intent on reaching the voices. What they saw now was that the sitting room was occupied, though the two people in it were off to one side and wouldn't have been visible by simply walking past the door.

Chief Morley sat in a stiff-backed chair, his arms tied behind his back, a rag stuffed into his mouth to stifle any words. An attractive, thirty-something woman stood over him, wielding a gun, which was pointed at Maggie and Sam.

"Natalie," Maggie whispered. The woman now sported blond hair and expensive-looking clothes.

"*John... get the hell in here with those two*," Natalie shouted toward the voices her eyes still on Maggie.

The tall, thin Amish man that had answered the door and a frightened pale woman in Amish clothes entered the room, trailed by a big burley man holding a second gun. Natalie waved her gun towards a sofa and Sam and Maggie moved towards it, and then sat gently down. Sam's eyes rested on the woman's gun, then moved to the burley man's matching weapon. He'd noticed a slight tremor in Natalie's hand, as if she weren't used to holding a heavy weapon.

Maggie's eyes were searching the room.

"Where is the boy?" she said. "*What have you done with that boy?*"

"Who the hell are you and why do you care?" John said. The look on his face silenced Maggie, but the frightened Amish woman spoke up, her voice urgent and pleading, her hands clutched together at her throat.

"He'll be home soon. You have to do something. They'll take my boy. They'll take him away. I waited so long, and then God gave us this miracle. *And now they want to take him away again!*"

"Shut up, you whining, sniveling fool. He wasn't yours in the first place," Natalie snarled.

The burly man, John Collins/Johann Becker, motioned for the pleading woman, who had to be Rebecca, and the tall thin man—Eli—to sit.

They sat in two stiff-backed chairs. John began to pace.

Natalie held her gun aloft, but glanced at her other arm, which sported a glittering watch.

"That kid better get here soon, John. Our plane leaves in an hour and a—"

The squeaking of the hinges at the front door cut her off mid-sentence, and a child's voice piped in.

"Mother, Father. You didn't come and get me. Mrs. Miller had to walk me home."

Six pairs of adult eyes looked towards the voice.

A boy of about seven strode through the entryway, then stood in the doorway of the sitting room. He was dressed in coveralls over a stiff woolen shirt. He carried a picture book and an old-fashioned blackboard slate. When he saw the adults, he stopped in his tracks. His eyes went from the Amish man and woman to John, whose body blocked most of Sam and Maggie from view.

"What are you doing here Mr. John? Why are you holding a gun?" he asked calmly. He only seemed surprised to see John; he was not frightened, just curious.

"Hello, Benjy. You've grown a lot. I've come to take you to your new home like I promised. Remember I told you this was just a resting place? Your new mom and dad can give you everything you could ever want. They're very rich and…"

Natalie cleared her throat.

"This is all very nice and cozy, but we have got to go. Grab the kid and let's hightail it, John."

Rebecca was now sobbing. "You can't do this, Johann," she cried. "Benjamin is ours now. You deserted him; we love him. Please don't take my boy."

Eli put his arm around his wife, pulling her close and trying to lend comfort. "I'm sorry, Rebecca," he whispered softly. "I never thought in a million years Johann would be this cruel."

Eli dropped his arm from around his wife, turned and faced his brother. "You hurt Rebecca once. I thought you had at least made up for that. How could you do this to us? Put down the gun. You're scaring Benjamin."

Natalie turned her gun on the couple.

"*We're going to do a lot more than scare him if you don't keep your yaps shut.*"

The child spoke in a strangely calm voice, a kind of singsong chant, as if he was dreaming or hypnotized. He looked only at John as he said, "Tell her to put the gun down, Mr. John. Guns are very dangerous. You know I'll come with you if you don't hurt anyone. Will you put down your guns?"

John stood frozen in place, a look of indecision on his face.

"*John, grab the kid and let's get out of here,*" Natalie screeched.

"I won't go with you if you don't put down the guns," the boy said, still not removing his eyes from John's face, not a trace of fear in his voice.

John looked from Natalie to the child, seemingly transfixed by the calm voice. He laid his gun carefully on a nearby table.

"Are you *nuts*? What the hell are you doing, John. Get your gun, get the kid, and let's *go!*"

Sirens sounded in the distance.

John simply motioned towards the front door, took the boy by the shoulder, and without forcing him, headed back through the entryway to the front door. Natalie began backing towards the sitting room doorway, her gun trained on the Beckers, the hand holding it trembling slightly. She got as far as the entryway and began to turn back around to head out the door.

Maggie and Sam had not moved from their seat on the couch, but Sam, spotting Rebecca heading for John's abandoned gun, began to rise from his seat.

"*You're not taking my child!*" the screaming Rebecca cried. She lunged towards the gun.

Natalie spun back towards the couple, her gun went off, and Eli crumpled to the ground.

For several seconds, everyone just looked stunned, including Natalie, who dropped the gun she was holding and bolted for the door. Rebecca fell to the floor, covering Eli's body with her own and beginning a keening moan.

"No, no, not my Eli. Not my Eli."

Sam was standing now. He took both guns, put one in his pocket and headed for the front door. He motioned for Maggie to stay in the room. She went to Chief Morley and began working on the ropes.

Sam knew he had to get to the departing threesome before they could escape in their car.

He stepped out onto the porch and raised his voice.

"Stop or I'll shoot."

Both John and Natalie froze in their tracks, but only for a moment. They made a snap decision to risk being shot for the sake of getting away, opened their cars doors, hopped in and started up the car. Sam shot at the tires, but missed. The car backed up, turned towards the lane and started down it, trailing a cloud of dust. Sam ran down the steps, ready to pursue them, but not willing to shoot towards the body of the car and risk hitting the child.

He could also see, however, that two police

cruisers turning into the lane would block their escape.

Sam was about to turn back towards the house, when he spotted a form on the ground struggling to stand and coughing from the dust. As it settled, Sam saw that the boy had somehow escaped being forced into the car and now stood, dazed, and seemingly unharmed.

Sam felt movement at his back.

"They didn't get him. They didn't get the boy," Maggie said, a note of joy in her voice. She walked down the porch steps and towards the child trailed by Chief Morley.

The boy began walking towards Sam and Maggie, but passed Sam and continued towards the house. As the boy and Maggie came close to each other, Maggie dropped to her knees and opened her arms. The child stood just in front of her, looking confused.

Then violet eyes met violet eyes, and a huge smile broke out on the child's face.

"I knew you would come, Mommy," Jenna Turner whispered. "I waited a long time, but I knew you would come get me."

CHAPTER THIRTY-ONE

AFTER TWO AND A half years away from home, Jenna Turner was sleeping peacefully in her own bed. The Beckers had been questioned, Eli from a hospital bed. They weren't arrested because it was clear to all involved the couple had no idea the youth they had taken into their hearts and home had been kidnapped.

The Collins didn't fare so well. John Collins was also in a hospital bed, but guards were posted outside his door. John had tried to escape through the fields and was stopped by a bullet. Natalie had not even tried. She'd given up easily once faced with six law officers, all armed.

It was almost a week after Jenna had been found, and Sam had gathered Maggie, Chad,

Casey, Danny, and Bob together to fill Jenna's parents in on the details.

They met at Maggie's home and were sharing coffee and cookies, which Maggie explained Jenna had proudly made herself.

"She's an amazing kid," Sam said as he crunched on the sweets. "I think Jenna is the heroine of her own story."

Chad looked puzzled. Maggie just nodded her head.

"She has a real instinct for survival and a giant heart," Sam continued. He took a sip of hot coffee and set the cup down gently on a saucer. He was seeing again in his mind the minutes following the discovery that Benjy was Jenna. After reuniting with Maggie, the little girl had followed the emergency responders into the home, then held Eli's hand and patted Rebecca on the shoulder as the medical team went to work. She obviously harbored no ill will against the couple that unwittingly held her captive.

"What's most astonishing to me is the bond she established with her kidnapper, John. I don't know whether it was her age or just her personality, but she was never afraid of him. He drugged her enough to get her to that cottage with little resistance, but we know that once she was there, she spent a couple of weeks with him."

At Maggie's anxious face, Sam rushed to add, "The doctor and psychologist both confirmed with authorities that he didn't touch her sexually, Maggie."

Maggie looked briefly at her own ceiling, sighed, and relaxed. Sam continued, "She was too young, really, to understand a lot of what was going on, and we can all be grateful she never sensed the danger she was in."

Sam cleared his throat and looked at Bob before opening a file on his lap.

"You see, when the police tracked down who John Collins—alias John or Johann Becker—is, we discovered he's a thug for hire. He's listed as a suspected killer, though he's never served time. He's wanted by the FBI for questioning about deaths in North Carolina and in Texas."

Maggie and Chad both gasped.

"Yet somehow your little girl stayed alive, even though we know now that John was supposed to kill her. Giving her to the Beckers was not part of the original plan. In fact, Natalie knew nothing about it until just recently."

Danny scratched his head and said, "Frankly, I'm most surprised that the God-fearing Beckers agreed to go along with anything Johann Becker proposed, especially this ruse that she was a boy. Did they think they could keep the fact she was a girl from the world?"

Sam was shaking his head.

"The FBI says they didn't know the child they took in was kidnapped and claimed they didn't know she was a she. John apparently coached Jenna in how to act like a boy; he also read to her from the Bible to teach her some of the Amish beliefs, and I think he convinced Jenna she was staying with the Beckers as Benjy for only a short while."

Maggie cut in, "From what Jenna tells us, John told her she had to wear the clothes he put her in and act the way he coached her to keep me safe from some great danger I was in. We know he told her that anyone who discovered the truth would be harmed, including the Beckers."

Sam referred to his notes.

"According to the interview report, the Beckers thought Jenna was Johann's own son, and they were desperate for a child. Even though Benjy came from a shunned brother, he was still blood. My guess is that they might have found out eventually, or maybe they just won't admit they knew Benjy was not a boy. They say Benjy convinced them he was old enough to bath himself, and the couple apparently let him."

Maggie shook her head, trying to take it all in.

"Why did John hatch this plan to keep her safe when he's killed other people?" she asked in a quiet voice.

"That's the really astounding part to me and I think to authorities as well," Sam said. He took a small bite of cookie and sat back to think.

"When authorities initially questioned him, he made it sound like it was never his intent to harm her, but he eventually broke down and admitted he couldn't do it. He said he even threw her into the water trying to drown her, but dove in after her himself to save her. She came up laughing, and he scooped her up and took her to shore."

Sam put down his cookie and leaned forward to look into Maggie's eyes and address her directly. "You saw how he was when we came to rescue Jenna. He put down his gun to get her out of there without a struggle. A suspected killer put down his gun. That's the really amazing part of this. I've never seen a child have such an effect on a hardened criminal."

Bob broke in on Sam at this point. "But two-and-a-half years? She never said anything in all that time!"

Sam leaned back to address the whole group.

"I'm no child expert, but remember how young she was when she was kidnapped. John may have convinced her not to say anything in the beginning out of fear, but I think she settled into the lifestyle and likely became what was expected of her. According to the therapist who examined her, Jenna was just waiting for the day when her mom was safe and could come get her. She knew she needed to play a role, but she remembered exactly who she was the minute she saw Maggie's violet eyes."

Those eyes now filled with glistening tears. One fat tear escaped to travel down her cheek.

"I can't believe she's safe. But then, I can't believe anyone, including Natalie – Nancy – would want to kill her. She's just a child."

Sam nodded his head.

"If Natalie had had her way, things would have gone much differently. She must have really hated you, Maggie. Not only did your dad help put her dad in prison, but you ended up with Chad."

Sam watched as Maggie's ex-husband reacted.

Did he actually puff up at the words?

"She did seem to fling herself at me in high school and even after that," Chad said. Maggie's fierce glare, however, poked a hole in his ego. His shoulders slumped, and his face colored.

Sam cleared his throat and continued, "Believe it or not, Natalie doesn't have a criminal record. John shows up in the database as a suspect for a number of crimes, including murder over the years, but he's always been a sticky fellow. He's never served jail time and kept slipping out of the grips of the law just before he was apprehended."

"Natalie must have been with him for years, but mostly in the background cheering him on. The initial kidnapping of Jenna, however, was her idea. We don't know yet if she just ran into you, Maggie, at Francine's, or if it was planned before then. It had to have made her even angrier, however, that you didn't even recognize her, though plastic surgery altered her face."

Maggie shook her head slowly, sighed, then wiped a hand across her face as if trying to wipe away the past. She straightened her shoulders.

"What did you find out about Kate, Sam?"

"Kate Morgan was reported as a runaway teen in 1989 by her mother Jane Morgan. Nothing ever came of it, though we confirmed Kate had run away and been returned several times before that. A couple years later, Jane Morgan reported her own brother missing, but I think police figured he'd moved without telling her."

"We now know that Kate and John lived in the same cabin where John kept Jenna and that Kate's uncle somehow tracked them down.

Killing him was the trigger that led John into crime, I believe. At least, it coincides chronologically. I don't think he cared about much after Kate was gone."

"Don't ask us to feel sorry for the creep," Chad piped in. He looked over at Sam, anger etched in the lines of his face. "He stole our kid and planned to kill her." The anger was replaced by curiosity. "How did they do it? How did the two of them manage to get Jenna away from Maggie?"

Bob took the lead on that question.

"Natalie got a copy of the key to the back door made during the few days the other clerk Trudy was in charge. On the day of the kidnapping, she let John in, and he hid in the dressing room. Then Natalie suggested to Jenna that the dressing room was a good place to hide. We know John used chloroform to subdue her and carried her away before anyone even knew she was gone."

He looked around at the group again, and then took a sip of coffee. Sam took over the explanation.

"We know John took Jenna to the cottage, but it was only supposed to be temporary, an isolated place he could reach on one or two tanks of gasoline. I suppose the original plan was to keep her there long enough to talk to you, Maggie and Chad, for proof she was alive. Then he was supposed to kill her, wait a couple weeks for the initial hub-bub to die down, and meet up with Natalie, who was in charge of collecting the ransom. I guess John trusted her enough to believe she wouldn't skip out on him."

"But where have they been these two and a half years since the abduction?" Casey asked. "Are they connected to the other kidnappings the FBI agent investigated?"

Sam and Bob exchanged looks. Sam sat back in his chair. It was Bob's turn to talk again.

"The cases aren't related. In fact, they don't know for sure, but it's possible none of them are. In the most recent case, they discovered the boy was taken by one of his babysitters—purely a money scheme gone badly. The babysitter was not a pro and chickened out. Fortunately, she convinced her boyfriend not to harm the boy, and he's back with his parents. The other Allentown case does not have a happy ending. They haven't been able to find the boy or trace the kidnappers down."

"Those poor parents," Maggie whispered. Her comment was echoed in the sad eyes of Casey, Danny, and even Chad.

Bob leaned forward to take a cookie, then sat back and took a bite. The action cut through the somber mood. Despite the seriousness of the discussion, the taste of the cookie put a small smile of pleasure on his face. He sighed contentedly before continuing.

"As for John and Natalie, they left the States several weeks after taking Jenna and went to Punta Mita, Mexico by plane. They stayed in a luxurious hotel at first, rubbing elbows with the people of the Mexican 'Riviera.' But they knew the $250,000 wouldn't last long, so they managed to find an isolated smaller hotel close to the same location. They apparently hobnobbed with some of the wealthy and occasionally stayed a week or so at luxury locations when they wanted to feel rich again, I guess. There were probably other small jobs along the way. They finally ran out of money completely and Natalie was the one to come up with their next scheme: stealing a child for another couple."

"But didn't you say Natalie didn't know about Jenna being among the Amish?" Maggie asked, her eyes wide.

Bob and Sam chuckled. Sam let Bob take the lead again on explaining why they were amused.

"During the interview with Natalie, we brought this up. At that point she lost it and changed her tune on John. She started saying things that are not going to help her husband's case with the courts. She was furious with him because getting rid of Jenna was the part of the plan he didn't stick to."

Sam took over there, explaining, "He apparently told her sometime during the end of their stay in Mexico, and plans switched to taking Jenna again and presenting her to the couple willing to pay $500,000 for a child, no questions asked. I don't think Natalie cared at that point what happened to the child. She just wanted money again."

All six adults took a moment to let that bit of information sink in. They sat sipping coffee, until Chad sat forward and asked, "What about Alfred Kulvert, the child molester. I can't believe he was living right across the street. Did you guys ever find that creep?"

Bob cleared his throat.

"His alibi for the period when Jenna was taken on their street was already pretty rock solid, but we did track him down, since he appeared to vanish close to the time of the kidnapping. The authorities caught up with him in Montana. He never went back to work for the firm that brought him here to your neighborhood; he didn't want to be found. He was still working construction, living in a remote location away from town. As far as the records show, he's never molested a child. But his dabbling in porn will follow him wherever he goes. He knows the authorities are watching him."

"And weren't you looking at the Stewarts, Sam?" Maggie asked.

Both Chad and Bob looked surprised at this revelation. It was Casey who answered the question. She was looking at the notes she'd brought with her.

"I looked into the Stewarts' background based on neighbor's comments about seeing a child there occasionally and a conversation Sam overheard."

All eyes turned to her.

"The Stewarts have a daughter who has severe developmental issues. She's living in a facility outside of Philadelphia. Mr. Stewart wanted to keep her there; Mrs. Stewart wanted her home. They settled on the occasional visit, but those visits have apparently lessened in frequency over the years as the daughter settled into the place where she lived. It was her home, and she didn't really react well to being uprooted even long enough for a visit."

Casey's face looked sad as she relayed this last piece of information. But the coffee was sipped, the cookies gone, and one by one the visitors got to their feet and said their good-byes. Chad grabbed for Sam's hand at the door.

"I guess I owe you thanks, Mr. Osborne. If

you and Maggie hadn't arrived when you did, I'm just not sure we'd have seen our Jenna again. I know you looked into me as a suspect, but I hope you know I would never have harmed a hair on her head."

Sam just stood nodding his head.

Then Chad looked over at Maggie, who was too far away to hear the two of them talking.

"Do me a favor and look out for her, okay? I know she thinks she's Miss Independent, but I think she needs a man in her life," he said.

Sam just smiled.

Chad shut the door behind him, and Sam grabbed for his coat.

"Stay for a while?" Maggie asked softly. The coat went back on the coat rack.

Maggie and Sam sat on the sofa, Sam's arm draped around Maggie's shoulder, her hand on his knee. She turned her head and kissed his cheek.

"Thank you," she whispered.

He leaned over and kissed her not so lightly and right on the mouth.

A giggle and footsteps on the stairs stopped him. The sound was music to Maggie's ears. Although her baby had come back to her seemingly unharmed, she was quieter and more mature. Maggie had missed almost two years of her daughter's life, and she occasionally felt like she was getting to know her child all over again. It was good to be reminded that Jenna was still a little girl.

Jenna bounded down the stairs and jumped onto the couch between them.

"Are you going to stay, Sam?" she asked, a big smile on her face.

"Is that okay with you?"

"Sure," she said, a note of excitement in her voice. "I think you're good for mommy. And I bet you're pretty good at Crazy Eights, too."

Sam laughed and looked into her violet eyes. Then he looked into the violet eyes of her mother. His eyes remained locked with Maggie's as he smiled and added, "Then I guess you better go get the cards."

EPILOGUE

EARLY THE NEXT SPRING

Sam sat alone sipping tea on Maggie's porch swing. The weather had just turned pleasant again, and a gentle breeze kissed his cheeks. It reminded him of the soft touch of the woman he'd spent so much time with lately.

He sighed and smiled contentedly, then laid his back against the board of the swing and soaked in the ambience. They deserved this break from the long, often hard months of this past winter. It had been a difficult time of police questioning, wrapping up details, court appearances, avoiding the media, and making adjustments to their lives.

But it had been less difficult than the anxious time leading up to it.

Maggie and Jenna had settled back into the routine of mother/daughter everyday life. It had taken the mother many weeks, therapy, and patience from Sam for her to stop hovering over her daughter, unable to let Jenna out of her sight for more than a few stressful minutes. Maggie could not fathom how her baby girl had weathered all the trauma of the over two years away and come back to her more mature and self-confident than when she left. The therapist declared the daughter less traumatized by those two-and-a-half years of absence than the mother was. Maggie gave the Beckers credit for some of that maturity—they had made Jenna feel safe, and they had taught her values that would likely stay with the little girl. But Maggie had trouble letting go of the fear that Jenna would disappear again, and Sam understood her caution. If he'd had a chance to get Davie back, he would have held on tight for a long time.

Sam helped Maggie adjust slowly. He was the first adult Maggie trusted to take Jenna out of the house alone. Sam and Jenna had just gone for ice cream—a small step on the road to recovery. Eventually, Maggie had begun to let her grip on the child ease. Jenna had been re-enrolled in school with extra help from a tutor to catch up on any schooling she hadn't received in her time with the Amish. And Maggie and Sam finally had time to pursue the relationship that began on the day they met, then took a few stolen passionate side trips, and finally took front seat in the journey of their lives.

The front screen door squeaked open and a gently smiling Maggie emerged.

"Sam."

Sam patted the seat of the swing and Maggie sat, drawing her legs up to her side onto the seat and snuggling up against Sam's strong shoulder.

"It's beautiful out today," she said softly.

"Indeed it is," he replied.

"Don't you have to get to work?"

"Yep. Casey made an appointment with a potential new client, but not until just before lunch. I'm getting there mentally first," he replied. "It's been a while since I've had a new case."

Maggie chuckled softly.

"You're a very good man, Sam Osborne. You've put your life on hold for too long."

"Indeed I have," Sam said, but he was smiling broadly. "It's been well worth it."

Maggie sat up and swung her feet to the floor. Sam glanced over at her, alert, as always, to her change in mood. She cleared her throat.

"Do you have a few minutes to talk, then?"

"Of course, Maggie. What's up?"

She turned her head to look at him, and then took his hand.

"I've just been thinking about us. About how much time we spend together."

"Yeah, I've noticed you can't get enough of me," Sam said, his eyes twinkling.

Maggie dropped his hand and slugged his shoulder, then got serious.

"Jenna loves you, you know."

Sam said nothing.

"And, well. I hope you know how much I love you, too. I hope I've let you know what a wonderful man I think you are."

Still, Sam said nothing.

"You've turned my life around. Not just by finding Jenna, but by showing me who I am. I've never felt more comfortable, or more fascinated by anyone in my life."

Sam was looking at his own lap, studying the back of his hands resting on his knees. Finally, he spoke, "I don't want to be just your warm and fuzzy or even just a good book you're enjoying."

"Oh, Sam," Maggie cried. She turned her body towards his on the swing, raised her palms and rested them on the sides of his face, then lifted his head so that he had to gaze into her eyes. "You also ignite a passion in me I have never felt. You are strong, loving, a good lover, a good friend."

Sam actually blushed at her words, making Maggie laugh again.

"And I think I've found my soul mate, Mister," she added.

The sentence lit Sam's eyes, then his entire face.

"Then marry me," he said, shocking Maggie enough that she dropped her hands. She turned and fell back against the porch swing again.

"I was going to suggest moving some of your things here," she squeaked.

"That can be arranged as well, Maggie. And I don't mean to push you. I know you've had a lot on your plate this year. I'm not in any hurry."

He turned and encircled her with his arms, drawing her close. His lips found hers and he took her breath away with his kiss. They stayed interlocked for several minutes, using their mouths to express their passion for each other until they both realized they were on the front porch. The seal was broken, and they sat back in their respective places on the porch swing.

"I'm not settling for just being your roommate. Just know that's my intention."

"Fair enough," she said. They laughed simultaneously and relaxed. Maggie took Sam's hand again. They sat in contented silence for several minutes.

Eventually, Sam turned to her again. He sensed the conversation wasn't over.

"Maggie?"

Maggie had been staring at their intertwined hands. She lifted them up briefly, then let them fall back to her lap.

"I want to share something with you. But I don't want you to think I'm an interfering old mom."

Sam's eyebrows rose.

Maggie sat forward far enough to reach into the back pocket of her jeans. She withdrew a sheet of paper.

"Jenna asked me to mail this for her," she said simply. She sat back again. "She had her counselor help her put it down on paper. I want your opinion on whether I should do as she asked and send it."

Sam's eyebrows rose again. Maggie began reading.

Dear Mr. John:

I don't like to think of you in jail. Is it like in the westerns with those metal bars? Do they make you sleep on the dirt floor? Are there rats? Can you see the sun?

They say that when you took me away, it wasn't to keep me safe or my mommy safe like you told me. I wouldn't believe them, except mommy and Poppa Sam say the same thing. And I don't think they lie. I don't think I know you so good, Mr. John.

I guess you might have lied. But I know in my heart you are not a bad man. You are just a sad man with a bad wife, maybe, and no little girl of your own to love. I saw sadness like that in Mother Becker's eyes a lot, but I could make her smile. I saw sadness in Father Becker's eyes, too, sometimes, but it was harder to make it go away. Mother and Father Becker didn't have a kid to love until you brought me to their house. So even though I missed my mommy like crazy while I was there, I'm not sorry I was part of your family for a while. You must have thought I was really special to bring me to your brother's house. And I know you brought me there because you knew Mother and Father Becker would take good care of me and love me.

But Mr. John, I am very happy now here with my mommy again and you should know that. And Poppa Sam is going to be another daddy for me, I just know that. He is always here and he makes me smile. He plays games with me all the time and he kisses my mommy. Some kids might think that's yucky, but I like it when her cheeks get red. I feel very happy to have them, as well as another daddy in town who I spent a whole week with over Christmas holiday. And guess what else!! Mommy and Poppa Sam are going to let me visit Mother and Father Becker this summer. So I can check on your brother for you. I guess Poppa Sam and Mommy know how it feels to miss a kid so much and they know Mother and Father are not bad people at all. They are good people with God in their hearts and dirt on their hands from so much hard work. And when I visit them, I'll get to visit my friends, Joshua and Hannah. I sure hope they don't think it's too weird I'm a girl instead of a boy. I didn't want to keep that secret, but I didn't want to get Mother and Father in trouble or make them sad I was a girl.

Mommy told me a sad story about you, too, Mr. John. She said you really loved a girl when you were young and that she was the girl that is buried at the cottage. Mommy said that when that girl got killed you got a disease in your heart. And then that disease grew really big and scary and maybe made you do bad things even when you didn't want to. I am sorry for you and for your sick heart, Mr. John. But it made me understand something. I was only a baby when we were at the cottage. And when the police asked me what happened, I told them the truth. That we played games and you taught me to be a boy and explained why being a boy was better for a while. I also told them how you looked at me funny a lot, but never were mean to me.

And I told them about your special name for me: Kate Eyes.

I hope you learn to like it there, Mr. John. I know how hard it is sometimes to make friends. Please know that I will think of you and wonder how you are doing.

Your friend,

Kate Eyes.

When she was done, Maggie sat back again, letting the letter fall to her lap. She ran one hand through her hair.

Sam took the letter and reread it.

"I see no reason not to send the letter, Maggie. John is in prison for many years. Jenna is an amazing little kid to even write this."

Maggie turned to Sam.

"I know. And I guess I agree it might not do any harm. But Sam… this man took my Jenna away for two and a half years. He took my baby away from me. He was supposed to *kill* her, Sam. How can I allow him any peace?"

Sam and Maggie sat in silence then. Sam refolded the letter and set it on the side table, then turned and took both of Maggie's hands.

"Maybe the point here, Maggie, is not what he was supposed to do, but what he really did do. I would have to assume that the fact she had Kate's violet eyes stopped him. But maybe it wasn't just her eyes that Jenna had. Maybe he got to know her well enough to realize she also had Kate's heart. Jenna was the best thing that happened to him since the last time he was at that cottage."

One of Maggie's hands came out of Sam's grasp and traveled to his face to outline its gentle contours.

"Sam Osborne, you're a very good man and I really love you a lot."

About the Authors

F. Sharon Swope

F. Sharon Swope began writing when she was ten years old and never stopped. Except for a weekly column in her local newspaper, Sharon never pursued getting her work professionally published. Instead, she married and focused her attention on her four children, all of whom became lovers of reading and writing.

At 82, Sharon realized that if she was ever going to write the books she had in her mind all those years, she had better get started.

Violet Fate is the third book she wrote in collaboration with her second daughter, Genilee. She is also coauthor of *Wretched Fate* and *Twist of Fate*. Sharon has published several short stories in magazines.

Sharon lives with her husband of sixty-four years, Robert, in Woodbridge, Virginia.

Genilee Swope Parente

Genilee Swope Parente has made her living writing and editing since she graduated in 1977 with a degree in Journalism from Ohio State University.

Since then, she has worked as a newspaper reporter, in public information offices for a university and a politician, and managed the periodicals for several trade associations. Currently, Genilee works as a freelance consultant writer, allowing her to edit and oversee magazines and newsletters for her clients.

In her free time, she can be found writing a book series for young adults while co-authoring the Sam Osborne detective series with her mother, F. Sharon Swope.

Genilee lives in Dumfries, Virginia with her husband of twenty years, Ray, and her teenage daughter Christina.

For more information about the
Sam Osborne series please visit
www.swopeparente.com

For more information about other titles available
from Spectacle Publishing please visit
www.spectaclepmg.com

CPSIA information can be obtained at www.ICGtesting.com
Printed in the USA
BVOW04s2243120215

387225BV00002B/2/P